Driven by that same little inner demon, Zoey moved a fraction closer, breathing in the vanilla-and-coffee scent of Finn's breath, her senses rioting.

"You think you're irresistible. That no woman with a pulse could ever say no to you. But I can resist you."

Finn touched his nose against hers—the tiniest nudge, but it sent a shock wave through her entire body. "You're not saying no to me—you're saying no to yourself. You want me so badly, I can feel it every time I see you."

Zoey fisted her hand in his hair in an almost cruel grip. "I didn't think it was possible to hate someone as much as I hate you."

His lips slanted in an indolent smile. "Ah, but you don't hate me, babe. You hate how I make you feel. And I make you feel smoking-hot."

"I feel *nothing* when I'm around you."

He gave a low, deep chuckle and placed his hands on her hips, tugging her forward until she was flush against his rock-hard body. "Then let's see if I can change that, shall we?"

Wanted: A Billionaire

What a woman wants...

Ivy, Zoey and Millie know what they want. They just never imagined that they might need the help of a billionaire to get it! Or that the arrival of Louis, Hunter and Finn would make their ordinary lives, in an instant, *extraordinary*!

Still, it's the ultrarich businessmen's worlds that will truly change. They're about to learn that life is about more than just their next business deal. This time, it's not their money that they'll have to put on the line... It's their hearts!

Lose yourself in...

Louis and Ivy's story
One Night on the Virgin's Terms

Millie and Hunter's story
Breaking the Playboy's Rules

And Zoey and Finn's story
One Hot New York Night

All available now!

Melanie Milburne

ONE HOT NEW YORK NIGHT

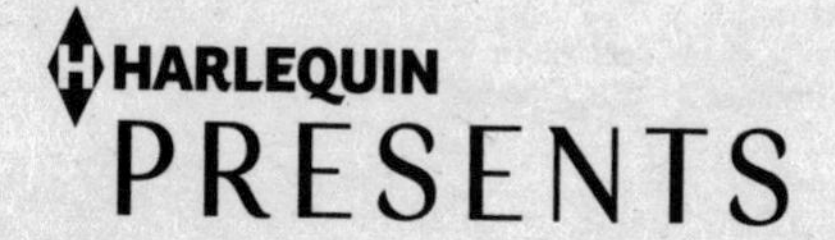

ISBN-13: 978-1-335-40405-3

One Hot New York Night

This edition published by arrangement with Harlequin Books S.A.

For questions and comments about the quality of this book, please contact us at CustomerService@Harlequin.com.

Harlequin Enterprises ULC
22 Adelaide St. West, 40th Floor
Toronto, Ontario M5H 4E3, Canada
www.Harlequin.com

Printed in U.S.A.

Melanie Milburne read her first Harlequin novel at the age of seventeen, in between studying for her final exams. After completing a master's degree in education, she decided to write a novel, and thus her career as a romance author was born. Melanie is an ambassador for the Australian Childhood Foundation and a keen dog lover and trainer. She enjoys long walks in the Tasmanian bush. In 2015 Melanie won the HOLT Medallion, a prestigious award honoring outstanding literary talent.

Books by Melanie Milburne

Harlequin Presents

The Return of Her Billionaire Husband

Conveniently Wed!

Penniless Virgin to Sicilian's Bride
Billionaire's Wife on Paper

Once Upon a Temptation

His Innocent's Passionate Awakening

Secret Heirs of Billionaires

Cinderella's Scandalous Secret

Wanted: A Billionaire

One Night on the Virgin's Terms
Breaking the Playboy's Rules

Visit the Author Profile page
at Harlequin.com for more titles.

CHAPTER ONE

ZOEY SAW HIM the moment she stepped into the London auditorium where the advertising conference was being held. It wasn't hard to make out Finn O'Connell in a crowd—he was always the one surrounded by drooling, swooning women. At six foot six, he was head and shoulders over everyone else, with the sort of looks that could stop a bullet train. And a woman's heart. An unguarded woman's heart, that was.

But, just this once, Zoey allowed herself a secret little drool of her own. She might hate him with a passion but that didn't mean she couldn't admire some aspects of him—like his taut and toned body, his strong, powerful, muscle-packed legs, his impossibly broad shoulders, his lean chiselled jaw or his laughing brown eyes. Other aspects, not so much. If there were an Academy for Arrogance, Finn O'Connell would be top of the class.

As if he sensed her looking at him, Finn turned

his head and glanced her way, his prominent black eyebrows rising ever so slightly above his eyes. Zoey was glad she wasn't easily provoked into a blush, as that mocking gaze moved over her in one slowly assessing sweep. His lips curved upwards in a smile that sent a frisson of awareness right through her body. It was the smile of a conqueror, a man who knew what he wanted and exactly how he was going to get it.

He moved away from his posse of adoring fans and strode purposefully in Zoey's direction. She knew she should whip round and dart out the nearest exit before he could get to her, but she couldn't seem to get her feet to move. It was as if he had locked her in place, frozen her to the spot with the commanding force of his dark brown gaze. She always tried to avoid being alone with him, not trusting herself to resist either slapping him or throwing herself at him. She didn't know why he of all people should have such an effect on her. He was too confident, too charming, too polished, too everything.

Finn came to stand within a foot of her, close enough for her to smell the expensive citrus notes of his aftershave and to see the devilish *ah, now I'll have some fun* glint in his eyes. 'Good morning, Ms Brackenfield.'

His bow and mock-formal tone stirred the hornet's nest of her hatred. The blood simmered in her veins until she thought they would explode. Zoey straightened her spine, steeled her gaze and set her mouth into a prim line. 'Looks like you've got your love life sorted for the next month.' She flicked her gaze in the direction of the group of women he'd just left, her tone rich with icy disdain.

His smile broadened and the glint in his eyes intensified to a sharp point of diamond-bright light that made something at the base of her spine fizz. 'You do me a disservice. I could get through that lot in a week.' His voice was a deep, sexy baritone, the sort of voice that made her think of tangled sheets, sweaty bodies, panting breaths, primal needs. Needs Zoey had ignored for months and would keep on ignoring…or try to, which was not so easy with Finn looking so damn sexy and standing within touching distance.

Being in Finn's company made her feel strangely out of kilter. Her usual *sang froid* was replaced with a hearty desire to slap his designer-stubbled face and screech a mouthful of obscenities at him. She raised her chin a fraction, determined to hold his gaze without flinching. 'One wonders if you have a revolving door on your bedroom.'

Finn's gaze drifted to her mouth, his indolent half-smile sending another frisson through her body. 'You're welcome to check it out some time and see for yourself.'

Zoey gripped the tote bag strap hanging off her

shoulder for something to do with her hands, her heart skipping a beat, two beats, three, as if she had suddenly developed a bad case of arrhythmia. 'Does that line usually work for you?' Honestly, if her tone got any frostier, they would have to turn on the heating in the auditorium.

'Always.' His lazy smile sent a soft, feathery sensation down the back of her neck and spine, and her willpower requested sick leave.

Zoey could see why he had a reputation as a playboy—he was charm personified in every line of his gym-toned body. But she *would* resist him even if it killed her. She stretched her lips into a tight, no-teeth-showing smile. 'Well, I'd better let you get back to your avid fans over there.'

She began to turn away, but he stalled her by placing his hand lightly on her wrist and a high-voltage electrical charge shot through her body. He removed his hand within a second or two, but the sensation lingered on in her flesh, travelling from her wrist, up her arm and down her spine like a softly fizzing firework.

'I was expecting to see your dad here. Or maybe I've missed him in the crowd.' Finn turned and scanned the auditorium before meeting her gaze once more. 'He mentioned in a text the other day about catching up for a coffee.'

Zoey couldn't imagine what Finn would have in common with her father other than they both ran advertising agencies. And as to having a coffee with him, well, if only it was caffeine her father was addicted to. It was no secret her dad had a drinking problem—he had disgraced himself publicly a few too many times in spite of her efforts to keep him from harming the business.

Brackenfield Advertising was her birthright, her career, everything she had worked so hard for. She would do almost anything to keep the business on track, which meant sometimes feeling a little compromised when it came to managing her father. And right now, her father was at home nursing yet another hangover. And it wasn't from indulging in too much caffeine.

'My father is…catching up on work at home today.'

'Then maybe you and I could grab a coffee instead.'

'I'm busy.' Zoey lifted her chin and narrowed her gaze to flint. 'I didn't know you and my father were bosom buddies.'

His lips quirked in an enigmatic smile. 'Business rivals can still be friends, can't they?'

'Not in my book.' Zoey pointedly rubbed at her wrist, annoyed her skin was still tingling. One thing was for certain—she would *never* be Finn O'Connell's friend. He was a player, and she was done with players. Done for good. She pulled her sleeve back down over her wrist. She hadn't been touched by a man in months. Why should Finn's touch have such an impact on her?

She couldn't deny he was potently attractive. Tall, lean and toned, with an olive complexion that was currently deeply tanned, he looked every inch the sophisticated, suave self-made businessman. Enormously wealthy, today he was casually dressed—as were most delegates—his crew-neck lightweight cotton sweater showcasing the breadth of his broad shoulders and his navy-blue chinos the length and strength of his legs.

But, while Finn looked casual, nothing about his approach to business was laid back. He was focussed and ruthlessly driven, pulling in contracts so lucrative they made Zoey's eyes water in envy.

Zoey could sense his sensual power coming off him in waves. She was aware of him as she was aware of no other man. She had known him for a couple of years or so, running into him at various advertising functions. He had been her only rival for an account a few months ago and it still infuriated her that he'd won it instead of her, mostly because she knew for a fact he had a friend on the board of directors of the company—a female friend.

'I hear you're pitching for the Frascatelli account,' Finn said with another mercurial smile. 'Leonardo Frascatelli is only considering three ad companies' pitches for his campaign. A battle between friends, yes?'

Zoey blinked and her stomach dropped. Oh no, did that mean he was vying for it too? With only three candidates in the running, she'd been confident she was in with a chance. But what would happen to her chance if Finn was in the mix?

The Italian hotel chain was the biggest account she had ever gone after, and if she won it she wouldn't have to worry about her dad frittering away the business's assets any more. She would finally prove to her father she had what it took to run the company. She ran the tip of her tongue over her suddenly carpet-dry lips, her heart beating so fast it threatened to pop out of her ribcage. She could *not* lose the Frascatelli account.

She. Could. Not.

And most certainly not to Finn O'Connell.

Zoey was flying to New York that evening to present it the following afternoon. Her presentation was on her laptop in the cloak room along with her overnight bag. Did that mean he was flying over there too? 'I can't think of a single set of circumstances that would ever make me consider being friends with you.'

'Not very creative of you,' he drawled, his gaze sweeping over her in an indolent fashion. 'I can think of plenty.'

Zoey gave him a look that would have sent a

swarm of angry wasps ducking for cover. 'I can only imagine what sort of ridiculous scenario a mind like yours would come up with—that is, of course, if you can get it out of the gutter long enough.'

Finn gave a rich, deep laugh that sent a tingle shimmering down her spine. Drat the man for being so incredibly attractive. Why couldn't he could have one just one physical imperfection? His mellifluous voice was one of the first things she had noticed about him. He could read out loud the most boring, soporific financial report and she would be hanging on his every word. His smiling dark brown eyes made her lips twitch in spite of her effort not to be taken in by his practised charm.

His mouth was nicely sculptured, his lips not too thick or too thin but somewhere perfectly in between. A mouth that promised erotic expertise in its every delicious contour. A mouth she had to keep well away from. No way was she joining the conga line to dive into his bed. No freaking way.

'I wouldn't dare to describe how my mind works.' He gave a slow smile and added, 'I might shock you to the core of your being.'

The core of her being was still recovering from his lazy smile, thank you very much. There was a fluttery sensation between her legs, and she hated herself for being so weak. So what if he was smouldering hot? So what if he made her feel more of a woman than she had ever felt just by looking at her with that sardonic gaze?

She *had* to resist him. She would be nothing more than a notch on his bedpost, a fleeting dalliance he would view as yet another conquest.

'Nothing about you would shock me, Finn. You're so boringly predictable, it's nauseating.' Not strictly true. He kept her on her toes more than any man she'd ever met. He constantly surprised her with his whip-smart repartee. She even—God forgive her—enjoyed their sparring. It gave her a rush, a secret thrill, to engage in a verbal scrap with him because his quick-witted mind more than matched her own.

Finn's eyes kindled, as if her carelessly flung words had thrown down a challenge he couldn't wait to act upon. 'Ah, well then, I'll have to lift my game to see if I can improve your opinion of me.' His lips curved in another smile that curled her toes inside her shoes.

'Finn!' A young blonde woman came tottering over in vertiginous heels with her hand outstretched, waving a business card held in her perfectly manicured fingers. 'I forgot to give you my number. Call me so we can catch up soon?'

Finn took the card and slipped it into his trouser pocket, his smile never faltering. 'Will do.'

The young woman looked as if she had just won the mega-draw lottery, her eyes so bright they could have lit up a football stadium. She gave Finn a fingertip wave and tottered back off to join her gaggle of friends.

Zoey rolled her eyes and, turning to one side, made vomiting noises. She straightened to lock gazes with Finn. 'Really?'

'She's an intern. I'm mentoring her.'

Zoey choked on a cynical laugh. She didn't know what annoyed her more—his straight face or his assumption she would be fooled by it. 'In the boardroom or the bedroom?'

His eyes never left hers, his mouth twitching at the corners with amusement. 'Your jealousy is immensely flattering. Who knew behind that ice maiden thing you've got going on is a woman so smoking-hot for me?'

Zoey curled her hands into fists, her anger flaring like a flame doused by an accelerant. It formed a red mist before her eyes and made each of her limbs stiffen like the branches of a dead tree. He enjoyed goading her—she could see it in his eyes. He liked getting a rise out of her and never wasted an opportunity to do so. He was playing her, and she was a fool to respond to him. But how was she supposed to ignore him? He wasn't the sort of man you could ignore. Oh, how she would love to slap his face. How she would love to kick him in the shins. How she would love to rake her nails—*her unmanicured nails*—down his face.

And, God help her, how she would love to sleep with him to see if he was as exciting a lover as gossip had it. Not that she would ever act on such a desire. Since being cheated on by her long-term boyfriend, Rupert, she was completely and utterly over men. She had given her all to her ex and had been completely blindsided by his betrayal. She didn't want the complications and compromises of a relationship any more.

But whenever she was anywhere near Finn O'Connell every female hormone in her body went into overdrive. She became aware of her body in his presence—of the tingles and flutters and arrows of lust almost impossible to ignore. But ignore them she must. Sleeping with the enemy was not in her game plan.

Zoey flashed him a livid glare, her chest heaving with the effort to contain her rage. 'I wouldn't sleep with you if you paid me a squillion pounds.'

His dark eyes danced and his confident smile irked her beyond endurance. 'Oh, babe, you surely don't think I'm the kind of man who has to pay for sex?' He stepped closer and placed two fingers beneath her chin, locking his gaze on hers. 'Can you feel that?' His voice lowered to a gravelly burr, his eyes holding hers in a mesmerising lock.

'F-feel what?' Zoey was annoyed her voice wobbled but her heart was leaping about like a mad thing in her chest, his fingers on her face sending a wave of scorching heat through her body.

Finn stroked his thumb over the circle of her chin, his warm minty breath wafting across her lips, mingling with her own breath like two invisible lovers getting it on. 'The energy we create together. I felt it the minute you walked into the room.'

No way was she admitting she felt it too. No way. Zoey disguised a swallow, her heart-rate accelerating, her inner core tingling as if he had touched her between the legs instead of on her chin. Why wasn't she stepping back? Why wasn't she slapping his arrogant face? She was under some sort of sensual spell, captivated by the feel of his thumb pad caressing her chin in slow strokes. Intoxicated by the clean, freshly laundered smell of his clothes, the citrus top notes and the sexy bergamot base note of his aftershave. She could feel the forcefield of his sensual energy calling out to her in invisible waves.

Her senses reeled from his closeness, his dangerously tempting closeness. She was acutely aware of his touch, even though it was only the pad of his thumb—it felt like a searing brand, the warmth seeping through her flesh travelling to her feminine core in a quicksilver streak.

Zoey had been celibate for months. She hadn't even thought about sex for weeks and weeks on end. Now, her mind was filling with images of being in bed with Finn in a tangle of limbs and crumpled bed linen, her body slick with sweat and glowing from earth-shattering pleasure. And she was in no doubt it would be earth-shattering pleasure. Being near him like this made her body pulse with longing—a raw, primal longing she wished she could block out, anaesthetise or bludgeon away. It was a persistent ache between her legs, a pounding ache in time with her heartbeat, an ache his touch triggered, inflamed, incited.

But somehow, with a mammoth effort, she got her willpower to scramble back out of sick bay. 'You're imagining it…' Zoey licked her lips and pulled out of his hold, rubbing at her chin and shooting him a frowning look through slitted eyes. 'If you ever put your hands on me again, I won't be answerable for the consequences,' she added through tight lips.

He gave a mock-shudder, his playful smile making his eyes gleam. 'Listen, babe, you'll be the one begging me to put my hands on you. I can guarantee it. *Ciao.*'

He walked away without another word and Zoey was left seething, grinding her teeth to powder, hating him all the more, because she had a horrible feeling he might be right.

CHAPTER TWO

FINN WAS STANDING in line waiting to go through the business class security checkpoint at London Heathrow airport when he saw Zoey Brackenfield two people ahead of him. He had sensed her presence even before he saw her—it was if something alerted him the minute he stepped into her orbit. It had been the same at the conference that morning—he had sensed her in the room like a disturbance in an electromagnetic field. A shiver had passed over his scalp and run down his spine, as if some sort of alchemy was going on between them—otherwise known as rip-roaring lust.

Finn always looked forward to seeing her at various advertising gigs. He enjoyed getting a rise out of her, which was amusingly easy to do. She was prickly and uptight, and flashed her violet gaze and lashed him with her sharp tongue any chance she got. But he knew deep in his DNA that underneath the prickly façade she was as hot for him as he was for her. Their combative repartee had been going on for months and he knew it was only a matter of time before she gave in to the desire that flared and flickered and flashed between them.

Zoey took out her laptop from its bag and put it on a tray to go through the scanner, her striking features etched in a frown. He noticed the laptop was exactly the same brand and model as his—even the light grey bag was identical. *Great minds think alike,* he mused, and stepped up to take a tray from the stack.

She placed her tote bag on another tray and stood waiting—not all that patiently. She shifted her weight from foot to foot, pushed back her left sleeve and glanced at the watch on her slim wrist, then pushed her mid-length silky black hair behind one shoulder. She was dressed in black leather trousers that clung like a glove to her long, slim legs and taut and shapely little bottom. Her silky baby-blue V-necked blouse skimmed her breasts and, when she turned on an angle in his line of vision and bent over to take off her high-heeled shoes, he caught a glimpse of her delightful cleavage and a jab of lust hit him in his groin.

As if she sensed his gaze on her, she straightened and met his gaze, her frown intensifying, her eyes narrowing, her lips pursing.

Finn smiled and pushed his laptop further along the conveyer belt, then he reached to unbuckle his belt to put it on the tray with his watch and wallet and keys. Zoey's eyes followed the movement of his hands as he slowly released his belt, and two spots of colour formed on her cheeks. But then she bit her lip and whipped back round as if she was worried he was going to strip off completely. If only they'd been alone, he'd definitely have done that, and enjoyed watching her strip off too.

There was a slight hold-up, as one of the people in front of Zoey had forgotten to take the loose coins out of their pocket. By the time Zoey walked through to collect her things from the conveyer belt, Finn's things had come through as well. She barely gave him a glance, and snatched up her laptop and tote bag and scurried off, but she was soon stopped by one of the random check personnel. She blew out a breath and followed the uniformed man to be electronically swabbed.

Finn absently put his laptop back in the carrier bag, his gaze tracking to Zoey as if drawn by an industrial-strength magnet. She was so damn cute he could barely stand it. But the people coming through behind him in the queue meant he had to get his mind back on the task at hand. He hitched the laptop bag over his shoulder then put his belt back on and slipped his wallet and phone and keys in his trouser pockets.

His gaze flicked back to Zoey and the frustrated look on her face brought a smile to his lips.

Those random checks were so random, he got called over every time he flew, but today was apparently his lucky day. No pat-down for him, but, hey, he wouldn't mind if it was Zoey doing the patting down.

Zoey was finally given the all-clear and gathered her things and stalked past, her head at a proud height, her gaze pointedly ignoring him.

'Got time for a drink?' Finn asked, catching up with her in a couple of easy strides.

'No, thank you. I don't want to miss my flight.' Even the sound of her heels click-clacking on the floor sounded annoyed.

'What flight are you on?'

She told him the carrier and the time, but it wasn't the same as his, and he was vaguely aware of a little stab of disappointment deep in his gut. Who knew what seven and a half hours in her company might have produced? He got hard just thinking about it.

'Good luck with your pitch,' he said with a smile. 'May the best person win.'

Zoey stopped walking to look up at him, her violet eyes like lethal daggers. 'If it were a level playing field, I would've won the last time we were pitching for the same account. Tell me, did you sleep with someone to swing the board's decision?'

'I don't have to resort to such tactics, babe, I just do a damn good job. Yours was a good pitch, though. And I really liked the dog food commercial you did a while back. Cute…real cute.'

She rapid-blinked in an exaggerated way, one of her hands coming up to her chest as if to calm her heart rate down. 'Oh. My. God. Did I just hear you give me a *compliment*?'

Finn chuckled at her mock-shocked expression. 'What? Doesn't anyone ever tell you how brilliant you are?'

'Not that I can remember.' She gave him a haughty look and added, 'But no doubt you've been hearing that said to you from the moment you were born.'

If only she knew how far from the truth that was. Finn had rarely seen either of his parents since he was six years old. They'd found the task of raising a child too restrictive for their hippy-dippy lifestyle—especially when he'd got to school age. They hadn't been able to handle the responsibility of waking up early enough after a night of drinking and smoking dope to get him ready for school or to pick him up afterwards, so they'd dumped him on distant relatives.

They had been given another couple of chances to get their act together during his childhood, but Finn had finally got tired of it by the time he was thirteen. He'd soon been shipped back to his relatives, who hadn't exactly welcomed him back with open arms. He couldn't recall too many compliments coming his way growing up, but he had got the message loud and clear that he'd been an encumbrance, a burden no one had wanted but kept out of a sense of duty.

'You'd be surprised,' Finn said with a hollow laugh.

Zoey looked at him for a beat or two longer, her forehead still creased in a slight frown. Then she shifted her gaze and glanced at her boarding pass. 'I'd better get to my gate…'

She walked off without another word and Finn felt again that strange little niggle of disappointment. He gave himself a mental shake and strode towards his own departure gate. He needed to get a grip. Anyone would think he was becoming a little obsessed with Zoey Brackenfield. He wasn't the type to get too attached to a woman—to anyone, when it came to that. His life in the fast lane left no time for long-term relationships. A long-term relationship in his mind was a day or two, tops. Any longer than that and he got a little antsy, eager to get out before it got too claustrophobic. Maybe he was like his freedom-loving parents after all. Scary thought.

It was almost three in the morning by the time Zoey got to her New York hotel. She had slept a little on the flight and watched a couple of movies rather than tweak her pitch on her laptop. She knew from experience that last-minute tweaks often did more harm than good. Her nerves would take over, her self-doubts run wild, and before she knew it the presentation would be completely different from her original vision.

Besides, she really loved travelling in Business Class. The way her father's business was currently going meant that travelling in style and comfort might not be something she would be doing too much longer, so she figured she might as well enjoy it while she could. No doubt Finn O'Connell had no worries on that score. She could just imagine him lying back on his airbed, sipping French champagne and chatting up the female cabin crew. *Grr.*

Zoey had a shower to freshen up and dressed in a bathrobe with her hair in a towel, turban-like, on her head, placing the laptop bag on the writing desk in the suite. She unzipped the bag and took out the laptop and laid it on the leather protector on the desk. She opened the screen and turned it on and waited for it to boot up. A strange sensation scuttled across her scalp as the screen became illuminated. She leaned forward, blinked her weary gaze and peered at the unfamiliar screensaver.

The unfamiliar screensaver...

Zoey's heart leapt to her throat, her legs went to water and her hands shook as though she had a movement disorder. This wasn't her laptop! She was in New York without her laptop. The laptop with her pitch on it.

Don't panic. Don't panic. Don't panic. She tried to calm herself down but she had never been a star pupil at mindfulness. Fear climbed her spine and spread its tentacles into her brain like a strangling vine. She was going to lose the contract. She was miles away from her laptop. What was she going to do? *Breathe. Breathe. Breathe.* Zoey took a deep lungful of air and stared at the laptop, praying this was a nightmare she would wake from at any moment.

But wait…all was not lost. Her presentation was in the cloud. But still, her laptop had a lot of personal information on it, and she didn't want to lose it. Besides, her pitch was first thing tomorrow morning and she couldn't be sure there would be another laptop she could use. And it would look unprofessional to turn up so ill-prepared.

Who owned this one?

Her mind spooled back to the security check at Heathrow and something cold slithered down the entire length of her spine. Could this be Finn O'Connell's laptop? Her stomach did a flip turn. Oh, no. Did that mean he had hers? She had a sticker on the back of her laptop with her name and number on it but there was nothing on the back of this computer.

The screensaver was asking for a password. She

drummed her fingers on the desk. Did she need a password to check if it was his computer? Maybe there was something in the laptop bag that might be enough of a clue as to whose computer it was. She reached inside the bag and took out a couple of pens and a collection of business cards. One, from a woman called Kimba, had a red lipstick kiss pressed to the back with a handwritten message below it:

Thanks for last night, Finn. It was unbelievable.

Zoey wanted to tear it into confetti-sized pieces and only just stopped herself in time. Double *grr.* What a player. He probably had lovers all over the world.

But at least it solved the mystery of whose computer Zoey had in her possession…or did it? The bag was the same as hers. No doubt there were other laptop bags exactly the same as this one. How could she know for sure this was Finn's computer inside his bag? It had been crowded at the security checkpoint and so many laptops looked the same. Besides, he hadn't phoned or texted her to tell her he had hers. Maybe someone else had hers and this was a complete stranger's!

Zoey searched further in the laptop bag and pulled out a bright orange sticky note attached to a computer technician's card. The sticky note had the words 'temporary password' written on it and below it a series of numbers and letters and dashes and hashtags. She stared at it for a long moment, a host of rationalisations assembling in her head. She needed to know for sure if this was Finn's laptop. She had a password but whether it was Finn's or not was still not clear. This could easily be some-one else's laptop accidentally put in his laptop bag.

She had to know for sure, didn't she? She had to check to see if it was actually Finn's laptop, right? She would call the airport once she knew one way or the other. She figured, if it turned out to be his, all she had to do was call him and ask him to meet her for a quick swap-over. There wouldn't be any delay that way, as he was probably in New York by now too.

Zoey stuck the note to the screen of the laptop and held her fingers over the keys. *You shouldn't be doing this.* She rolled her left shoulder back-wards, as if she was physically dislodging her nagging conscience. Her fingers moved closer to the keyboard and her heart began to thud, a fine sweat breaking out across her brow. She could only imagine how nauseating it would be to read his emails. No doubt hundreds of gushing messages from his many lovers telling how wonderful he was. Could she stomach it? No. Definitely not.

Zoey got up from the desk, folding her arms across her body to remove them from temptation.

It would be wrong to read his personal messages—anyone's, for that matter. Was it even a crime?

But then a thought crept into her brain… Could she just click on Finn's pitch? Just a teensy-weensy little peek? No. That would be taking things a little too far. She was a morally upright citizen. She believed in doing the right thing at all times and in all circumstances. And yet…this was her chance to get a heads-up on what his pitch looked like. He would never know she'd checked…

But *she* would know, and that was something that didn't sit well with her. The competition had to be fair and equal and, if she looked at his pitch and made last minute changes to hers once she got her laptop back and subsequently won the account, how victorious would she actually feel? It would be a hollow victory indeed. She wanted to win the pitch on her own merit. She had fought too hard and for too long to be taken seriously. If she were to cheat to get to the top, then she would be devaluing everything she had worked so hard for.

Zoey glanced back at the laptop, her teeth chewing at her lower lip. 'You can stop looking at me like that, okay?' She addressed the laptop sternly. 'I'm not doing it. I would hate it if he did it to me.'

Yikes! But what if he was doing it to her at this very moment?

Zoey let out a stiff curse. Those last few emails she sent to her ex were not something she wanted anyone else reading, and certainly not Finn O'Connell. She walked back to the computer and slammed it shut. 'There. Who said I can't resist temptation?'

As long as she could resist Finn O'Connell just as easily.

After dinner was served and then cleared away on the flight, Finn took out his laptop and set it up before him in his business class seat. But as soon as he opened it he knew something wasn't right. For one thing, there were food crumbs all over the keys, which was strange, because he never ate at the computer. Besides, it had only just come back from his tech service people, who had serviced one of his faulty programs, and they always returned it spotless.

He pressed the 'on' button and an unfamiliar screensaver came up. Shoot. He had someone else's laptop.

Someone who had gone through the security check at the same time.

He turned the computer over and found a sticker on the back with Zoey's name and number on it. A smile broke over his face and he closed the laptop with a snap. What were the chances of them switching laptops?

As much as he was tempted to have a little snoop around Zoey Brackenfield's laptop, he was going to resist. Who said he couldn't be a chivalrous gentleman? She had a right to her privacy; besides, he could do without any more animosity from her. He genuinely liked her. She was feisty, determined and talented, and he admired her all-in work ethic. She was in a still largely male dominated field, but she didn't let it intimidate her. A couple of her projects he'd seen had been nothing short of brilliant.

Finn showered and shaved once he got to the penthouse suite of his hotel. He had yet to call Zoey about the laptop mix-up, but considering it was the middle of the night he figured it could wait until a decent hour. Clearly, she hadn't discovered the mix-up because he had no missed calls or text messages from her.

He had got a text message from Zoey's father, however, mentioning something about a business matter he wanted to discuss with him. Finn couldn't decide if it was one of Harry Brackenfield's increasingly regular drunken, middle-of-the-night texts or if there was a genuine reason behind his request for a meeting. Either way, it could wait. He had much more important business on his mind—getting his laptop back and seeing Zoey again.

But as Finn was coming out of the bathroom his phone buzzed from where he'd left it on the bedside table earlier. He walked over to scoop it up and saw Zoey's name come up.

'Good morning,' he said. 'I believe have something of yours in my possession.'

'Did you do it deliberately?' Her tone was so sharp, he was surprised it didn't pierce one of his arteries. 'Did you switch them at the airport?'

Finn walked over to the windows to look at the view of the city that never slept. The flashing billboards and colourful lights of Times Square were like an electronic firework show. 'Now, why would I do that? It's damned inconvenient for one thing and, secondly, dangerous to have my personal data in the hands of someone who doesn't have my best interests at heart.'

'I want it back. Now.' Her tone was so strident and forceful, he could almost picture her standing in her hotel room visibly shaking with anger.

He let out a mock-weary sigh. 'Can't it wait until morning?'

'It *is* morning,' she shot back. 'Where are you staying? I'll come to you right now.'

'Now is not convenient.'

There was a silence in which all he could hear was her agitated breathing.

'Have you got someone with you?' Zoey asked.

'You might not believe this but I'm all by myself.' Thing was, he was all by himself more often than not just lately. He was the first to admit his sex life needed a reboot. The hook-ups were not as exciting as they used to be. None of his lovers captivated him the way he wanted to be captivated. The way Zoey captivated him. His focus on her was stuffing up his ability to sleep with anyone else. But that was easily fixed—he would convince her to indulge in a hot little hook-up. Problem solved.

Zoey made a scoffing noise, as if in two minds whether to believe him about his solitary status. 'Then there's no reason I can't come by and get my computer and give you yours.'

'Why can't you wait until a decent hour? Or are you worried I'm going to hack into your computer, hmm?'

There was another tight little silence, punctuated by her breathing.

'Y-you wouldn't do that…would you?'

Finn let out an exaggerated sigh. 'Your low opinion of me never ceases to amaze me. Look—I'll compromise and bring your laptop to you rather than you come out in the wee hours. Where are you staying?'

She told him the name of the hotel, which was only a block away. 'How long will you be?' she added.

'Don't worry, babe. I know you're impatient to see me, but I won't keep you waiting much longer.'

'It's not you I want to see, it's my computer.' And then the phone clicked off.

* * *

Zoey tugged the damp towel off her head and threw it on the bed, her fury at Finn knowing no bounds. She wouldn't put it past him to have deliberately switched their computers. He never failed to grasp an opportunity to get under her skin. No doubt he'd been trawling through her emails and photos and pitch presentation without a single niggle of his conscience. She, at least, had felt conflicted enough not to do it, even if it had been a close call in terms of self-control. She shut down his computer and put it back in the laptop bag and firmly zipped it up.

But deep down she knew she had made the choice not to snoop because she respected him professionally, even if she had some issues with how he lived his private life.

Or maybe her issues with his private life were because she was envious of how easily he moved from one lover to the next. She had been unable to stomach the thought of sharing her body with anyone since her ex had cheated on her. Well, apart from Finn, which was both annoying and frustrating in equal measure, because he was the last person she wanted to get naked with under any circumstances. However, it was a pity her body wasn't in agreement with her rational mind.

The doorbell sounded before Zoey had time to

change out of the hotel bathrobe into clothes. She clutched the front opening of the bathrobe together and padded over to the door. 'Is that you, Finn?'

'Sure is.'

Zoey opened the door and found him standing there with her laptop bag draped over one shoulder. He didn't look one bit jet-lagged—in fact, he looked ridiculously refreshed and heart-stoppingly gorgeous. He had recently showered and shaved, his brushed back thick, dark hair still damp. The tantalising notes of his aftershave drifted towards her, reminding her of a sun-baked citrus orchard with crushed exotic herbs underfoot. She held out her hand for her computer. 'Thank you for dropping it off. I won't keep you.'

He held firm to the laptop resting against his hip, one prominent dark eyebrow rising in an arc. 'Aren't you forgetting something?'

Zoey looked at him blankly for a moment. He flicked his gaze towards the writing desk behind her, his expression wry. 'I'll give you yours, if you give me mine. Deal?'

Zoey was so flustered at seeing him at this ungodly hour and looking so damn hot, she'd completely forgotten she had his computer. 'Oh…right, sorry…' She swung round and padded over to the desk to pick up the laptop. But then she heard the soft click of the suite door close behind her and a tingle shot down her spine. She turned to face him, her pulse rate picking up at the sardonic look in his eyes. 'I don't remember asking you into my room.'

'I know, and it was most impolite of you to not at least offer me a drink, since I walked all this way in the dark to bring you your laptop. I could have been mugged.' His eyes had a devilish gleam and her pulse rate went up another notch.

Zoey gave him a look that would have withered a plant. A plastic plant. 'Fine. What do you want? Erm, to drink, I mean.'

She was in no doubt about what he really wanted. She could see it in eyes, could feel it in the air—a throbbing pulse of sexual energy that pinged off him in waves, colliding with her own energy, stirring a host of longing and need that threatened to consume her. She felt it every time she was in his presence, the dark, sensual vibration of mutual lust. It horrified her that she was in lust with him. Horrified and shamed her. How could she possibly think of getting it on with him? He was a playboy. A man who had a freaking turnstile on his bedroom door. It was lowering to admit she was so attracted to him. What sort of self-destructive complex did she have to lust after a man she didn't even like?

'Coffee. I'll make it.' Finn sauntered over to the small coffee percolator near the mini-bar area. His take-charge attitude would have annoyed her normally, but she was tired and out of sorts, and the thought of someone else making her a coffee was rather tempting.

'Fine.' She sank to the small sofa in front of the television, wondering if she should have put up more of a fuss and insisted on him leaving. She realised, with a strange little jolt, she had never been totally alone with him before. There had always been other people in the background such as at conferences or at the airport the previous day.

One thing she did know—being alone with Finn O'Connell was dangerous. Not because he posed a physical threat to her safety but because she wasn't sure she knew how to handle such a potently attractive man at close, intimate quarters. At six-foot-six, he made the hotel room seem even smaller than it actually was. And, while she was no midget at five-foot-ten, she was currently barefoot and wearing nothing but a bathrobe.

Being so minimally attired made her feel at a distinct disadvantage. She needed the armour of her clothes to keep her from temptation. And temptation didn't get any more irresistible than Finn O'Connell in a playful mood.

Within a short time, the percolator made its gurgling noises, and the delicious aroma of brewed coffee began to tantalise Zoey's nostrils. Finn poured two cups and brought them over.

'Here you go. Strong and black.'

Zoey frowned and took the cup from him. 'How did you know how I take my coffee?'

His eyes twinkled. 'Lucky guess.'

Her lips twitched in spite of her effort to control her urge to smile back at him. The last thing she wanted to do was encourage him…or did she? The thought trickled into her head like the coffee had done in the machine just moments ago.

The dangerous thought of exploring the tension between them hummed like a current. It was a background hum, filtering through her body, awakening her female flesh to sensual possibilities. Possibilities she had forbidden herself to consider. Finn was a player, a fast-living playboy who had 'heartbreaker' written all over his too-handsome face. She had already had her heart broken by her ex. Why would she go in for another serve? It would be madness…

But it wouldn't be madness if she set the terms, would it? Why shouldn't she allow herself a treat now and again? She had given so much to her ex and got nothing back. Why not indulge herself this time with a man who didn't want anything from her other than hot no-strings sex?

Finn picked up the writing desk chair and placed it close to the sofa where she was sitting. He sat on the chair and balanced his right ankle over his other thigh in a casual pose she privately envied. Zoey had never felt more on edge in her life. Edgy, restless...excited. Yes, excited, because what woman wouldn't be excited in Finn's arrantly male presence?

Zoey sipped her coffee, covertly watching him do the same. Her eyes were drawn to the broad hand holding his cup, her mind conjuring up images of those long, tanned fingers moving down her body...touching her in places that hadn't seen any action for months on end. Places that began to tingle as they woke up from hibernation.

She sat up straighter on the sofa, almost spilling her coffee. 'Oops.' She caught a couple of droplets rolling down the side of her cup before they went on the cream linen sofa.

'Too hot for you?' Finn asked with an enigmatic smile, his eyes glinting.

You're too hot for me. Zoey put her cup on the lamp table next to the sofa, her hand not as steady as she would have liked. 'No, it's fine. I'm just jet-lagged, I guess.'

He leaned back in his chair until it was balanced on the back legs only, his gaze measuring hers. 'Did you sleep on the plane?'

Zoey nodded. 'I'm glad I did now. If I'd realised you had my computer on the plane, I would have been in a flap of panic. It was bad enough finding out when I did, but at least it was only for a short time.'

There was a pulsing silence broken only by the

sound of his chair creakily protesting at the way it was balanced. Finn rocked forward and the front legs of the chair landed on the carpet with a thud. 'So, how did you figure out it was my computer?'

'There was a business card in the laptop bag with a lipstick kiss on it from a woman called Kimba.' She picked up her coffee with a roll of her eyes. 'I'm surprised there was only one card. I was expecting hundreds.'

He gave a laugh and leaned forward to place his coffee cup on a nearby table. 'I do clean it out occasionally. But that wasn't all that was in the bag.'

Zoey brought her gaze back to his. 'You're crazy for leaving your password on a sticky note. What if someone else had got your laptop?'

His mouth curved upwards in a smile, making his eyes crinkle attractively at the corners. 'I had my laptop serviced yesterday and they reset the password. I haven't had time to reset it again.' He reached for his coffee cup, took a small sip and then balanced it baseball-style in his hand. 'So, did you read my emails? Have a little snoop around?'

Zoey could feel heat storming into her cheeks and put her coffee back down on the table. 'Of course I didn't. Did you read mine?'

He placed his hand on his heart. 'Scout's honour, I didn't. I was tempted, sure, but I figured it was a pretty low thing to do.'

She bit down on her lower lip before she could

stop herself. For reasons she couldn't explain, she believed him. He might be a charming player in his free time, but he was scrupulously honest in business. He had built from scratch an advertising empire that was one of the most successful in the business. She might not like him, but she couldn't help admiring him for what he had achieved.

Finn took another sip of his coffee. 'Did you look at my pitch?' His eyes held hers in a penetrating lock that made her scalp prickle.

Zoey sprang up from the sofa as if one of the cushions had bitten her on the bottom. 'I admit I was tempted, seriously tempted, but I didn't do it. Besides, I already know you're going to win.' She was doomed to fail with him as an opponent. It was galling to think he was going to win over her yet again. Would she ever get a chance to prove herself? She drew in another breath and released it on a defeated sigh. 'I think I haven't got a chance against you.'

'Come now, it's not over till it's over.' He got up off the chair and placed his coffee cup on the table with a loud thwack. 'You haven't even presented yours and you're giving up? What sort of attitude is that in this business? You have to believe in yourself, Zoey, no one else will if you don't.' His tone sounded almost frustrated, a frown deeply carved on his forehead.

His unexpected reaction surprised Zoey into a defensive mode. She curled her lip, her eyes flashing. 'Thanks for the pep talk, O'Connell. But I don't need you to tell me how to live my life.'

He raked a hand through his hair, leaving track marks amongst the thick strands. 'Look, I know things are a little messy with your father right now. But…'

Messy? She didn't need Finn to tell her how messy things were—she lived the cringeworthy reality every single day. Watching her father go from hero to zero, picking him up after every binge drinking session, covering for him when he missed a deadline, making excuses to clients when he failed to show up for a meeting… The list went on. Zoey tightened her arms around her middle until she could barely breathe. 'I'd like you to leave. Right now.'

Finn held her stormy gaze with unwavering ease. 'I admire your father. In his day, he was one of the best in the business but—'

'Get. Out.'

'I'd leave if I thought that's what you really wanted.'

Zoey thrust up her chin, her eyes blazing, her body trembling with forbidden longing. A longing she was desperately trying to control. 'Oh, so now you're an expert on what I want? Don't make me laugh.'

Finn stepped up to within a few centimetres of her, not touching her but standing so close she could see the detail in his eyes—the tiny flecks of darker brown like a mosaic, the pitch-black rim of his irises as if someone had traced each circumference with a felt-tip marker. He said nothing, did nothing, his expression almost impossible to read except for a diamond-hard glint in his eyes. Her eyes drifted to the sensual contour of his mouth and something deep in her core fluttered like the wings of moth—a soft, teasing reminder of needs she had ignored for so long. Needs Finn triggered in her every time she was near him, erotic needs that begged to be assuaged.

Zoey became aware of the heat of his body, aware of the energy crackling in the small distance between their bodies. *Touch him. Touch him. Touch him.* The mental chant sounded in her head, the need to do what her instincts demanded a relentless drive she suddenly couldn't control. Her hands went to the rock-hard wall of his chest, her fingers clutching at his T-shirt until it was bunched in both of her hands.

One part of her brain told her not to get any closer, the other part said the exact opposite. The push and pull was like a tug-of-war in her body. She was drawn to him like an iron filing to a powerful magnet, the sheer irresistible force of him overwhelming any blocking tactics on her part—if she could have come up with one, that was. Her rational mind was offline, and her body was now dictating the way forward. It had taken control and was running on primal instinct, not on rationality and reason.

One of her hands let go of his T-shirt and went to the back of his head. She stepped up on tiptoe and got her mouth as close to his as was possible without actually touching it. She didn't know why she was flirting so recklessly with danger. She didn't know why she was putting herself so close to temptation when her ability to resist him was currently so debatable.

But some wicked little imp inside her egged her on to see what would happen. She knew it was dangerous, infinitely dangerous, but oh, so wickedly thrilling to have him teetering with her on a high wire of self-control, not sure who was going to topple off first.

Her heart was beating like a tribal drum, the same erotic rhythm that was pulsing insistently between her legs. 'You think I can't wait for you to kiss me, don't you? But do you know what's going to happen if you so much as place your lips on mine?'

Finn still didn't touch her; his hands were by his sides but his hooded gaze communicated the effort it took not to do so. 'I'm going to kiss you back like you've never been kissed before, that's what.' His voice was deep and husky, his sensual promise sending a shiver cartwheeling down her spine.

Driven by that same little inner demon, Zoey

moved a fraction closer, breathing in the vanilla and coffee scent of Finn's breath, her senses rioting. 'You think you're irresistible. That no woman with a pulse could ever say no to you. But I can resist you.'

Could she? Maybe, but why did she have to? They wanted the same thing—no-strings sex, an exploration of the lust that flared between them. What could be wrong with indulging her neglected senses in a simple hook-up with him?

Finn nudged his nose against hers—the tiniest nudge, but it sent a shockwave through her entire body. 'You're not saying no to me, you're saying no to yourself. You want me so badly, I can feel it every time I see you.'

Zoey fisted her hand in his hair in an almost cruel grip. 'I didn't think it was possible to hate someone as much as I hate you.'

His lips slanted in an indolent smile. 'Ah, but you don't hate me, babe. You hate how I make you feel. And I make you feel smoking-hot.'

'I feel *nothing* when I'm around you.' *Liar, liar, pants literally on fire.* On fire with lust.

He gave a low, deep chuckle and placed his hands on her hips, tugging her forward until she was flush against his rock-hard body. 'Then let's see if I can change that, shall we?' And his mouth came down firmly, explosively, on hers.

CHAPTER THREE

ANY THOUGHT OF pushing him away flew out of Zoey's head the moment his mouth crashed down on hers. Besides it being too late, deep down she knew she had intended this to happen from the get-go.

She wanted him to kiss her.

She wanted to push him over the edge.

She wanted him to be as desperate for intimate contact as was she.

His lips were firm, insistent, drawing from her an enthusiastic response she hadn't thought herself capable of giving to a man she didn't even like.

But what did like have to do with lust? Not much, it seemed.

The sensual heat of his mouth set fire to hers, his tongue entering her mouth with a bold, spine-tingling thrust that made her inner core contract with an ache of intense longing. His tongue duelled with hers in an erotic battle that sent her pulse rate soaring. She kissed him back with the same fierce drive, feeding off his mouth as if it was her only source of sustenance. Never had a kiss tasted so good, felt so good. It made every cell in her body throb with excitement.

One of Finn's hands went to the small of her back, drawing her even closer to his pelvis. The rigid press of his erection sent another wave of longing through her body. She made a sound at the back of her throat, a desperate whimpering sound of encouragement, and pushed further into his hardness, her arms winding around his neck, her fingers delving into the thickness of his hair.

Finn tilted his head to gain better access to her mouth, one of his hands cupping the side of her face. His tongue flicked against hers, calling it back into play, teasing her to a point where she was practically hanging off him, unable to stand on her own, for her legs were trembling so much. Never had she felt such ferocious desire. It pounded through her with each throbbing beat of her blood.

The taste of his mouth, the texture of his skin against her face, the feel of his hands on her hip and her cheek, sent her senses sky-rocketing. She needed to be closer. Ached to be closer. Would die if she didn't get closer.

Zoey unwound her arms from around his neck, tugging his T-shirt out of his jeans and placing her hands on his muscled chest, still with her mouth clamped to his. Her tongue danced with his in a sexy tango that made hot shivers go down her spine like a flow of molten lava.

Finn lifted his mouth off hers, looking at her with his dark, mercurial gaze. 'How am I doing so far? Have I changed your mind, or shall I stop right now?'

'Shut up and keep doing what you're doing,' Zoey said, dragging his head back down so her mouth could reconnect with his.

The kiss went on and on, more and more exciting, more and more intense, leaving her more and more breathless, aching with want and wondering why the hell she had rebuffed him earlier. *This* was what she wanted. This passionate awakening of her senses, catapulting her into a maelstrom of delicious feeling. Feelings that she had forgotten she could feel but which she was feeling now even more intensely than ever before.

Finn lifted his mouth off hers only long enough to haul his T-shirt over his head, tossing it to one side before his lips came back down on hers with fiery purpose. His breathing was heavy, the primal, growling sounds he made in his throat ramping up her own arousal. One of his hands slipped between the front opening of her bath robe to claim her left breast. She gasped at the contact of his hands on her naked flesh, her body erupting into flames.

'Yes...oh, yes...' Zoey hadn't realised she had

spoken out loud until she heard the sound of her desperate plea. 'Don't stop.'

Finn's eyes blazed with lust and he brought his mouth down to her breast, circling her nipple until it rose in a tight bud. He took it in his mouth, sucking on her with surprising gentleness, the sensation sending her senses spinning out of control. She grasped at his head, her spine arching in pleasure, her lower body tingling, tightening in anticipation of his intimate possession.

He lifted his mouth off her breast and held her gaze in an erotically charged lock that made the backs of her knees tingle and flames leap in her feminine core. 'I want you.' His bald statement was the most exciting, thrilling thing she had ever heard.

'Yeah, I kind of guessed that.' Zoey rubbed against him, shamelessly urging him on. 'But I don't want to talk. I want to do this.' She placed her mouth on his chest, circling her tongue around his hard, flat nipple, delighting in the salty taste of his skin. She began to go lower, drawn to the swollen length of him, driven by some wicked force within her. She had to taste him. *All* of him.

Finn made a rough sound at the back of his throat and captured her by the upper arms. 'Wait. I have other plans for you right now.'

He ruthlessly tugged the bath robe fully open, sliding it down her arms and untying the belt so it dropped to the floor at her feet. His hungry gaze devoured every inch of her flesh but, instead of shrinking away from him, Zoey stood under his smouldering gaze, relishing every heart-stopping moment of seeing the raw, naked lust on his face. She was empowered by the way he was looking at her, as if she was some sort of sensual goddess that had materialised before him. She was giddily excited by the rampant desire she triggered in him—the same out-of-control desire he triggered in her.

'I want to see you naked. Fair's fair.' Zoey surprised herself with her boldness. Who was this wild and wanton woman blatantly stating her needs?

Finn held her gaze with his smouldering one. He unsnapped the stud button on his jeans and rolled down the zipper, the *zzzrrruuppt* sound sending a shiver skating down her spine. He stepped out of his jeans, and then out of his black form-fitting undershorts, and her heart rate went off the charts.

Zoey sucked in a breath, devouring every proud inch of him with her gaze. 'Mmm…not bad, I suppose.'

Finn gave a laugh and grasped her by the hips again, tugging her against his potent heat. 'I've wanted to do this for months.' He began to nibble on her earlobe, the teasing nip of his teeth making her shudder with pleasure.

'So, let's do it.' Zoey could hardly believe she was saying it, but it was all she wanted right now. *He* was all she wanted right now. To have his potent, powerful body ease the desperate, clawing ache of her female flesh.

Finn pulled back a little to look into her eyes with a searching expression. 'Are you sure this is what you want?'

Zoey rubbed up against him again, her gaze sultry, delighting in the way he snatched in a breath as if her body thrilled him like no other. 'I want you, Finn. I don't know how to make that any clearer.'

'While we're on the topic of clarity—you know I'm not in this for the long haul, right? I don't do long-term relationships. It's not my gig—never has been, never will be.'

Zoey stroked her hand down his lean jaw. 'Yes, well, that's lucky, because I don't either. Or at least, not any more.' She stroked the length of his nose and then outlined the contour of his mouth and added, 'This is exactly what I need right now. A one-night stand with a man who won't call me tomorrow and want a repeat.' She tapped his lower lip with her fingertip. 'Deal?'

Something shifted at the back of his gaze—a tiny flicker, like a sudden start of surprise, but quickly concealed. 'Deal.' His mouth came down to hers in a hard, scorching kiss, the heat inflamed all the more by the erotic press of their bodies.

Zoey opened to the commanding thrust of his tongue, her arms winding around his neck, which brought her tingling breasts tighter against his chest. The sprinkling of his chest hair tickled her soft flesh and his guttural groan as he deepened the kiss made her toes curl into the carpet at her feet. She had never felt such overwhelming desire for a man, such intense longing, it consumed her from head to foot.

Finn walked her backwards to the bed, his mouth still pressed firmly against hers. He laid her down and stood looking at her for a long, breathless moment, his body in full arousal making her inner core coil and tighten with lust.

Being taller than most of her friends, Zoey had her share of body issues, always feeling gargantuan compared to her petite friends. But with Finn's ravenous gaze moving over her she felt like a supermodel and, for the first time in for ever, proud of her feminine curves and long limbs. 'Had your fill?' she asked in a coquettish tone.

'Not yet.'

He leaned down over her, resting his hands either side of her head, his gaze capturing hers. 'You're beautiful—every delicious inch of you.'

'Yes, well, there are quite a few inches of me.'

He smiled and stroked a lazy finger down between her breasts, his eyes darkening to pitch. 'And I am going to kiss each and every one of them.'

Zoey shivered, her need for him escalating to the point of discomfort. She reached up to grasp his head with both of her hands. 'If you don't have sex with me soon, I'm going to scream.'

His brown eyes glinted. 'Then it looks like I'm going to make you scream either way.'

A frisson passed over her body at the erotic promise of his statement, the same erotic promise she could see in his eyes. She had never been all that vocal during sex with her ex. Their love life had become a little routine over the time they'd been together, but she had put that down to the increasing demands of their careers. If she were to be perfectly honest, it had even been a tad boring at times.

'I'm not a screamer, as it turns out.' Zoey wasn't sure why she was spilling such personal information to him.

Finn came down beside her on the bed and placed his hand on her mound. 'Then I guarantee you soon will be.'

He brought his mouth down to her folds and she arched her spine like a languorous cat, unable to speak for the sensations flowing through her. Electric sensations sent ripples of pleasure to every inch of her body. His tongue stroked against the swollen bud of her clitoris, delicately at first, gauging her response, before he increased his rhythm and pressure.

Zoey gasped as lightning bolts of delight coursed through her flesh, the tension building inexorably to a point of no return. A part of her mind drifted above to look down at her body being pleasured by Finn, and was a little shocked at how vulnerable she had made herself to him. The intimacy of what he was doing to her was way beyond what she had experienced before. Rupert had occasionally gone down on her, but he never stayed long enough for her to feel anything more than a few vague flutters.

But with Finn her body was on fire, and the flames were licking at her flesh with tongues of incendiary heat. Zoey arched her spine even further, her legs trembling as the wave of pleasure hit her with a booming crash. Her breathless whimpers became cries, and then an almost shrill scream, as the waves kept coming, one after the other, pummelling her, pounding through her, until she was thrown out the other side, limp, satiated, in a total state of physical bliss.

'Oh, dear God…' She was lost for words, her breathing still out of order, her senses still spinning.

Finn moved back up her body, his eyes shining like dark, wet paint. 'Ready for more?'

'You can't be serious? I'm a come-once-only girl.'

A wicked glint appeared in his gaze. 'Let's see what I can do about changing that.' He sprang off the bed and went to get a condom from his wallet in the back pocket of his jeans. Zoey relished watching him, his gloriously naked body stirring a new wave of longing in her. He tore the foil packet with his teeth, tossing away the wrapper, and then rolled the condom over his erection, glancing at her with that same dancing, devilish glint in his eyes. And Zoey almost climaxed again on the spot.

Finn came back over to her and she reached up and tugged him back down so he was lying over her, his weight balanced on his arms, one of his powerful thighs hitched over hers. He leaned down to kiss her and she tasted herself on his lips, the raw and earthy intimacy of it blowing her mind. His tongue entered her mouth, teasing hers into a duel that mimicked the throbbing energy of him poised between her thighs. He ran one hand down the flank of her thigh in a slow stroke, and then back again, his mouth moving against hers with deeper and deeper passion.

He lifted his mouth off hers to gaze down at her, his breathing heavy. 'I don't think I've ever wanted someone more than I do you at this moment.' His voice was rough-edged, his eyes holding hers in an intimate lock that heralded the sensual delights to come.

Zoey placed her hand at the back of his head, her fingers toying with his hair. 'I bet you say that to everyone you sleep with.' Her tone was teasing but a part of her realised with a twinge of unease—their one-night stand agreement notwithstanding—she didn't want him to look on her as he looked on his other lovers. She wanted to stand apart, to be someone who wouldn't just disappear into the crowd of past lovers, the nameless women he had pleasured and then walked away from without a backward glance. The sort of women who gave him business cards with lipstick kisses and 'thanks for the memories' messages.

But exactly what *did* she want?

Zoey didn't want a committed relationship with Finn, or with anyone else for that matter. That part of her life was over. Dead and buried. She could never trust another man, let him into her life, into her body and then find he had betrayed her. She wasn't that much of a fool to lay herself open again to such ego-shredding hurt.

But she did want to feel alive and, right now, she had never felt more so.

Finn brushed a wayward strand of her hair back off her face. 'I haven't said it to anyone and meant it the way I do right now. You drive me crazy.'

'You drive me crazy too.'

'Good, because I would hate it if things weren't equal between us.' He nudged at her entrance, his eyes darkening as he surged into her with a throaty groan.

Zoey gasped in bliss as he drove to the hilt, her body welcoming him, wrapping around him, gripping him as he started thrusting. She was quickly swept away with his fast-paced rhythm, her senses reeling as the friction increased. Sensations shot through her female flesh, darts, flickers and arrows of pleasure that increased with every deep thrust of his body. She gripped him by his taut buttocks, unable to think, only to feel. And, oh, what exquisite feeling. Tingles, fizzes and starbursts of pleasure rippled through her. The tension grew and grew in the most sensitive nub of her body, but she couldn't quite tip over the edge.

Finn brought his hand down between their bodies and began to stroke her swollen flesh with his fingers, the extra friction, right where she needed it, sending her into outer space. Her orgasm was like a meteor strike exploding in her flesh, sending ripples and waves and rushes of pleasure through her body so fast and so furiously, it was almost frightening. Her body had never felt so out of control. It was spinning and thrashing and whirling with sensations that went on and on, the sweet torture making her throw her head back and bite back a scream.

The muffled scream turned into a sob—a laughing sob of disbelief. How could she have experienced such a tumult of the senses with a man she viewed as the enemy?

Finn gave another deep groan and surged deeply, his movements fast, almost frantic, before he finally let go. Zoey gripped him by the buttocks, a vicarious frisson of pleasure passing over her body as she felt the intensity of his release. He collapsed over her, his breathing still hectic, the slightly rougher skin of his jaw tickling her cheek.

After a few moments, he propped himself up on one elbow to look down at her, his body still joined to hers. He brushed back a stray hair from her face, his expression difficult to make out. His eyes moved between hers, back and forth, back and forth, every now and again dipping to her mouth and back again. He brought his index finger to her mouth and tapped her gently on her lips. 'You rocked me to the core.'

'I'm not finished rocking you.' Zoey captured his finger with her teeth, biting down with just enough pressure to see his pupils flare. She opened her bite just enough so she could glide her tongue over the pad of his finger, holding his smouldering gaze.

'Whoa there, babe. I have some business to see to.' He sucked in a breath and pulled away to deal with the used condom.

Zoey lay on her side with her elbow bent, resting her head on her hand, and followed him with her gaze, drinking in the sight of his lean, tanned build and firm muscles. 'Do you have any more condoms with you?' She could barely believe she had asked such a question. Who was this insatiable woman? It was certainly nothing like her former self.

Finn winked at her and picked up his wallet. 'Enough.'

'How many is enough?'

He walked back over to her and sat beside her, one of his hands running up and down her leg. 'What time's your pitch?'

Zoey glanced past him at the bedside clock and her stomach nose-dived. How could so much time have passed? She had completely forgotten about her pitch at nine a.m. 'Oh, shoot. I have to rush.' She brushed his hand away and scrambled off the bed, grabbing the bath robe off the floor and bundling herself into it. 'I have to shower and do my hair and make-up.' And get her scattered senses under some semblance of control.

Finn rose from the bed with an inscrutable look on his face. 'Then I won't keep you any longer.'

Zoey stood toying with the belt of her bath robe as he dressed, her teeth chewing at her lower lip, her body still tingling from his intimate possession. He picked up his laptop bag and slung it over his shoulder, his expression still masked.

'Erm…thanks for bringing me my laptop,' Zoey began but found herself floundering for what else to say. *Thanks for the memories? Thanks for giving me the best two orgasms of my life? Can I see you again?* No. She definitely was *not* saying that.

No way. She had scratched the Finn O'Connell itch and it was time to move on. 'Hope you have a good flight back home,' she added. Urgh. Of course he would have a good flight home, no doubt with the Frascatelli account firmly in his possession.

Finn gave a brief smile that didn't reach his eyes. 'It was my pleasure.' And then he walked out of the suite and closed the door behind him with a definitive click that made Zoey flinch.

CHAPTER FOUR

FINN'S PITCH PRESENTATION didn't go as he'd envisaged. For one thing, his mind was replaying every moment of making love to Zoey Brackenfield instead of focussing on selling his vision for the ad campaign to the client's representative.

The second thing was a niggling sense of irritation that Zoey hadn't expressed a desire to see him again for a repeat session or two. He had expected her to say it before he left her hotel room. Expected it so much that when it hadn't been forthcoming it had stung him in a way he had not been stung before. It was ironic, as usually it was he who sent a lover on her way with no promise of a follow-up. But it was her call, and he had a feeling it wouldn't be long before their paths crossed once again. And he would make the most of it.

The sex had been nothing short of phenomenal, a totally mind-blowing experience, and he wanted more. Ached to have her in his arms again with a throbbing ache so deep and intense, it was distracting him from his work. So much so, he didn't realise the representative from the Frascatelli Hotel corporation was speaking to him.

'I'm sorry,' Finn said. 'I missed that last bit. What did you say?'

The representative closed their meeting with a stiff smile. 'Once Leonardo Frascatelli has a look at the three candidates' presentations for himself, and my order of preference, he will make a final decision and be in touch on who gets the contract. It will be a few days, I should think.'

'Thank you.' At least he might be in with a chance if Leo Frascatelli had the final say, Finn thought with an inward sigh of relief. It was a big account, and he knew there would be ongoing work once this initial campaign was over. He liked to win when he set his mind on a goal. It was why he loved the advertising business—it was an adrenalin rush, a fast-paced creative process with big dividends. He enjoyed the team work and he had some of the best in the business working for him.

But the biggest adrenalin rush he'd experienced lately was his one-nighter with Zoey. The hunger she had triggered in him hadn't gone away in spite of their hot night of sex. It hadn't defused anything. Instead, his hunger for her was even more ravenous than before. She stirred a fervent sexual energy in him, an energy unlike anything else he had experienced with anyone else.

He didn't know what it was about her, but he wanted more. Zoey had said she hated him, but it didn't change the fact that she desired him. And what a scorching-hot desire it was. He shuddered every time he thought of her silky warmth gripping him so tightly, her breathless gasps and cries of pleasure, the almost desperate clutch of her hands on his body. He had felt the same desperation to be as close as it was physically possible to be.

Finn walked out of the meeting room, sure he could pick up a faint trace of Zoey's perfume lingering in the air from when she had pitched earlier that morning. He closed the door on his exit and blew out a long breath.

Boy, oh, boy, did he have the lust bug bad.

Zoey flew back to London later the same day, determined to stick to the plan of no repeats of her completely out-of-character hook-up with Finn O'Connell. But the deed was done and now it was time to move on and not allow herself to think of him. Anyway, he was probably in bed with someone else by now.

As for her pitch, well, it was Finn's fault she had stumbled and garbled her way through it like a rookie intern on her first project. How was she supposed to perform at a peak professional level with her body still tingling from head to foot from Finn's off-the-scale lovemaking?

But then a thought dropped into her head… Maybe that had been his plan right from the start. Maybe he had wanted to sabotage her pitch by scrambling her brain, short-circuiting her senses, until all she could think about was the stroke and glide of his hands on her skin, his powerful body deep within hers, the star-bursting orgasms that had left her body still tingling even hours later.

Maybe even the laptop switch had been deliberate. Seeing him in the queue at Heathrow had certainly flustered her. She had been so intent on getting through security without betraying how much he unsettled her, she had grabbed a computer off the conveyor belt without properly checking if it was hers.

But, as much as she was annoyed with herself over that little mix-up, how could she regret sleeping with him? It had been more hate sex on her part than anything else, but it had totally blown her mind and sent her senses into haywire from which they had yet to recover. How could she regret having the most incredible sex of her life?

Erm…because it's Finn O'Connell?

Zoey closed her eyes in a 'why was I such an idiot?' manner. But she consoled herself that it was only the once and it would not be repeated. There was no way she was going to hanker after him like his posse of fan girls. She had way too much pride.

In fact, she was not going to think about him at all.

Finn had only been back at his office a few minutes when his receptionist-cum-secretary, June, informed him Harry Brackenfield was waiting to speak to him in the conference room. 'He said it's highly confidential and he didn't want to be seen waiting for you in the waiting room,' she added. 'He wouldn't even make an appointment to come back at a more convenient time.'

'That's okay, I'll see him,' Finn said, wondering if he was in for a lecture about sleeping with Harry's daughter. But surely Zoey wouldn't share such private details of her love life with her father? Besides, Harry Brackenfield didn't seem the devoted and protective dad type.

Harry's attitude to Zoey troubled Finn at times. He had overheard Harry at a cocktail party a couple of months ago denigrating a project Zoey had worked on early in her career. Personally, Finn had thought her early work showed enormous talent. It had been a little rough around the edges but that was normal for a newbie. Her later work was nothing short of brilliant, but he had a feeling she wasn't allowed to shine too brightly at Brackenfield, in case her work eclipsed her father's.

Finn walked into the conference room to find Harry seated on one side of the long table, his hands clasped together.

'Morning, Harry,' he said, taking the seat at the head of the table. 'I missed you at the conference the other day. I thought we were going to have coffee to discuss something.'

Harry's eyes shifted to one side. 'Yes, well, I thought it was too public there to discuss what I want to discuss with you.' His gaze moved back to Finn's. 'I want out.'

Finn frowned in confusion. 'Out?'

Harry separated his hands and laid them on the table. Finn noted both of them had a slight tremble. 'I'm offering you a takeover of Brackenfield Advertising. I know you've done takeovers in the past, and I thought you might be interested, since you've been asking me over the last couple of months about how things were going. I'm done. I'm tired of the long hours and my creativity has dried up. I want to take early retirement.'

A tick of excitement ran through Finn's blood. A friendly takeover was the ideal way to acquire a company, but it concerned him that Zoey hadn't mentioned anything about it during their time in New York. And it begged the question as to why. 'Does Zoey know about this?'

A dull flush rose on the older man's cheekbones. 'No. And I insist the deal is off if she's told before the deal is signed off. It's my company and if I want to sell it, then I'll sell it. This is an exclusive offer to you but, if you don't want it, then I'll offer it to someone else.'

The trouble was, Finn did want it. Brackenfield Advertising would be a nice little coup to add to his empire, but it didn't sit well with him that Zoey was in the dark about the takeover. But business was business and, since Harry was the owner and director, what else was Finn supposed to do? Confidentiality was a cornerstone of good business deals and he wanted that company before one of his competitors got it.

Besides, his one-night stand with Zoey was exactly that—a one-night stand. Even if part of him wished it could be repeated. Would this takeover ruin the chances of seeing Zoey again? A niggle of unease passed through him, but he forced himself to ignore it. He wasn't interested in anything long-term even if Zoey was the most exciting lover he had been with in years...possibly ever.

Finn made a generous offer and readily Harry accepted it. It seemed to confirm the older man's keenness to do other things with his life other than work.

'Right, then, it looks like you've got yourself a deal,' Finn said, rising from his seat to offer Harry his hand. 'I'll get my legal people in contact with yours to get the paperwork written up.'

Harry shook Finn's hand. 'Thank you.'

Finn waited a beat before asking, 'Why the secrecy from Zoey? Surely as your only daughter she has the right to know what your plans are going forward?'

Harry's expression became belligerent. 'If she were my son, then maybe it would be different. But she's not. She'll get married and have kids one day soon and then what will happen to the company?'

'Men get married and have kids too and still successfully manage companies,' Finn felt compelled to point out, even if he didn't place himself in that category. The marriage and kids package had never appealed to him, mostly because he had seen first-hand the damage when it didn't work out. 'Anyway, isn't Zoey more a career woman? That's the impression I've always had when speaking with her.'

It was weird because Zoey reminded him of himself—career-driven, single and wanting to stay that way, yet up for a bit of no-strings fun now and again to relieve the tension. The only trouble was, he didn't like the thought of her having fun with anyone else. If she wanted to have fun, then he wanted to be the one to have it with her. For now, at least. Not for ever.

'I'll tell her as soon as the deal is done and dusted,' Harry said. 'And not before.'

'Your call, but I think you're making a big mistake.'

Harry narrowed his eyes. 'Since when have you been such a champion for my daughter? She hates your guts, or haven't you noticed that small detail?'

Finn suppressed a smile. 'Let's say we've been working at our differences.' And having a hot lot of fun doing it too.

'Hey, how did your pitch in New York go?' Millie, one of Zoey's previous flatmates, asked at their bridesmaid dress fitting a few days later. 'I meant to ask you earlier, but I've been distracted by things...'

'Things' being Millie's recent engagement to hot-shot celebrity lawyer Hunter Addison. Madly in love, Millie had already moved out of their flat to live with him. Ivy Kennedy, Zoey's other previous flatmate, had also moved out a few weeks ago to live with her fiancé, Louis Charpentier. They were getting married next month, and Zoey and Millie were both going to be bridesmaids. And, when Millie and Hunter got married a couple of months after that, Ivy and Zoey would be maid of honour and bridesmaid, along with Hunter's young sister, Emma.

'I haven't heard back yet,' Zoey said, twirling from side to side in front of the full-length mirror in the bridal store's fitting room. 'I don't think this shade of blue suits me.'

'Are you nuts?' Millie laughed. 'You look stunning in it. And it really makes your violet eyes pop.'

What had made Zoey's eyes pop was seeing Finn O'Connell naked in her hotel room. Even though she had insisted their hook-up be a one-off, it still rankled a bit he hadn't called or texted her since. It was perverse of her to hope for a repeat when she had been the one to issue the once-only terms.

'I don't know…' She swished the long skirt of the dress from side to side, her mind wandering back to how it felt to have Finn's hands gliding over her naked body…

'Hey, earth to Zoey,' Millie said. 'You've got such a far-away look in your eyes. Did something happen while you were in New York?' She waggled her eyebrows meaningfully. 'Like with a man, for instance?'

Zoey flattened her mouth and frowned. 'What on earth makes you think that?'

Millie's face fell at her sharp tone. 'Sorry. Is it your father, then?'

Zoey let out a serrated sigh. 'I didn't mean to snap at you, it's just…'

'Tell me.' Millie touched her on the arm, her expression concerned. 'Has your dad been binge drinking again?'

'I haven't seen him since I got back from New

York, so I don't know, but on balance I would say probably he has been.' She chewed at her lip and then added, 'I had a one-night stand.'

Millie's eyes went so wide, they could have moonlighted as Christmas baubles. 'Seriously? Who was it? How did you meet? What was it like? Will you see him again?'

Zoey twisted her mouth and fiddled with the shoestring strap of the bridesmaid dress. 'I'll probably see him again, but not like that.' She met her friend's eyes in the mirror. 'It was Finn O'Connell.'

Millie frowned. 'Your competitor for that other project? But I thought you hated him.'

Zoey gave her a wry look. 'Yes, well, it wasn't so long ago that you hated Hunter Addison and look where that led.'

Millie's expression was sheepish but glowing with happiness too. *'Touché.'* But then her frown came back. 'Are you saying you *feel* something for Finn O'Connell?'

'Of course not!' Zoey laughed. 'What a crazy question to ask.'

'You must have felt something otherwise you wouldn't have slept with him. You haven't had a date since you broke up with Rupert. Finn must have made you feel something to—'

'I felt lust.'

'And now?'

Zoey unzipped the dress. 'And now, nothing. It was a one-night stand and I don't want to repeat it.'

'Was it that bad?'

'Unfortunately, no.' Zoey sighed and stepped out of the dress and hung it back on the padded hanger. 'No wonder that man has a conga line of women waiting to fall into bed with him.'

'That good, huh?'

'Indescribable.' Zoey stepped into her jeans and pulled up the zip. 'But I'm not getting involved with a playboy.'

'They make wonderful fiancés once they fall in love,' Millie said. 'You only have to look at Louis and Hunter to see that. You couldn't ask for a more devoted partner. Did I tell you Hunter is helping my mother with her literacy problems? He's so patient with her, and I love him all the more for being so wonderfully supportive.'

'Hunter is a one-in-a-million guy and I'm happy for you.' Zoey reached for her top and pulled it over her head, then shook out her hair. 'But I'm not interested in a long-term relationship. Been there, done that, thrown away the trousseau.'

Millie gave her a long, measuring look. 'I know Rupert broke your heart cheating on you the way he did. But you can't stop yourself from falling in love with someone again out of fear. I wake up each day feeling so blessed I found love with

Hunter. It would be so wonderful to see you happy again too.'

'Yes, well, maybe I wasn't all that happy with Rupert,' Zoey said, slipping her feet back into her shoes.

It was slowly dawning on her that her relationship with her ex had had some serious flaws which she had chosen not to notice at the time. It was sleeping with Finn O'Connell that made her realise how boring and routine things had become with Rupert. But, rather than address it at the time, she had blithely carried on until it had got to a humiliating showdown, finding him in bed—in *their* bed—with another woman.

'But you were with him for seven years.'

'Yeah, don't remind me,' Zoey said, rolling her eyes. 'I wished I'd left before he made such a fool of me.' She blew out a breath and added, 'I think I got too comfortable in my relationship with him. He told me he loved me daily and I believed it, more fool me. I should know by now you can never trust a word a man says.'

'Not all men are like Rupert.'

'Maybe not, but you only have to look at my father to see he's cut from the same cloth,' Zoey said. 'Says one thing, does another. He told me he was going to rehab the last time we had dinner. But did he do it? No. And lately he's been avoiding me. Ignoring my texts and not answering my calls. I should be relieved at the reduced contact with him, but I know him well enough to know he's up to something he knows I won't approve of. Fingers crossed it's not a new lover young enough to be his daughter. Urgh.'

'Oh, Zoey, I'm sorry you've been let down so much by your dad. But losing your mother when you were so young must have really devastated him.'

Zoey hated being reminded of the loss of her mother when she'd been only four years old. One day her mum had been there, the next she wasn't. Carried away in an ambulance after falling from her horse while Zoey had been at kindergarten, dying three days later from severe head injuries, never having regained consciousness. Zoey hadn't had the chance to say goodbye. She hadn't even been allowed to go to the hospital or to the funeral. Her father had insisted she stay at home with the hastily engaged nanny—one of many, along with various stepmothers who had come and gone during her childhood.

'Yes, well, I lost her too, and do you see me drinking myself into a stupor and making a complete and utter fool of myself? Besides, his drinking has been a fairly recent thing. His last marriage break-up with his wife Linda seemed to be the trigger. She was the first woman he really cared about since mum. Another good reason not to fall in love. It's not worth it.'

Millie sighed. 'I'm sure your mum would be so proud of how you watch out for your dad and of all you've achieved professionally.'

Zoey picked up her tote bag from the chair. 'Yes, well, all I've achieved will be for nothing if I don't get this contract. Come on. I need a coffee.'

All this wedding preparation stuff was seriously messing with her head. Her two best friends had fallen in love with wonderful men—even a hardened cynic like her had to admit Hunter Addison and Louis Charpentier were worth giving up singledom for. But she had been so stung by Rupert's betrayal, and wondered if she would ever allow herself to trust a man again. She had given so much to her relationship with him, been there for him in every way possible, only to find it had all been for nothing. How could she open herself again to such excruciating pain and humiliation?

Finn was in his home office a couple of days later reading through the now mutually signed takeover contract Harry Brackenfield's lawyer had sent via courier. There was a cooling off period of a week, but he knew Harry wouldn't back away from the deal—not with the eye-watering amount of money Finn had paid. But Finn had made plenty of money over his career and the odd gamble now and again wouldn't harm the coffers. Brackenfield Advertising needed a thorough overhaul and a bit of dead wood would have to go. It was a business, after all, and a business was all about profit. That was the bottom line.

Finn's rescue cat, Tolstoy, was sitting on his desk with a scowl on his face. The battle-scarred Russian blue hadn't quite forgiven him for leaving him with the housekeeper when he flew to New York. Tolstoy had pointedly ignored him for the first three days and now, on day five, was only just softening towards him, in that he now tolerated being in the same room as him.

Finn slowly rolled a pen across his desk. 'Go on, you know you want to.' The pen rolled in the direction of the cat's paw, finally coming to a stop against a paperweight, but all Tolstoy did was give him an unblinking stare.

'Still mad at me, huh?' Finn opened the top drawer on his desk and took out a length of string and dangled it in front of the cat's face. 'What about this?'

Tolstoy continued to stare at him, his one green eye nothing short of scathing.

'You know something?' Finn said, dropping the string back in the drawer and closing it. 'You remind me of someone. She looks at me just like that.' He went back to the paperwork on his desk, reading through the fine print with studied concentration… Well, it would have been a lot easier to concentrate if his mind hadn't kept drifting to Zoey.

His phone buzzed beside him on the desk and he picked it up with a quick glance at the screen. It wasn't Zoey but Leo Frascatelli, which could only mean good news. 'Finn O'Connell.'

'Finn, I have a proposition for you,' Leo said. 'I've had a look at the three pitches and I've chosen you and Zoey Brackenfield as equal first. I couldn't choose between you, so I want you to work together on the campaign. Is that doable?'

It was doable but was it wise? Finn hadn't seen her since New York and with each day that had passed the ache to do so had got worse. It was so out of character for him to be hankering after a follow-up date with a lover. Working with Zoey would bring her back into his orbit but it would ramp up the temptation to sleep with her again. And again. And who knew how many more times? He wasn't normally one to mix business with pleasure. But he was prepared to risk it because the Frascatelli project was a lucrative one even if the profits would be split two ways.

'Sure. Have you talked to Zoey yet?'

'Not yet. I thought I'd run it by you first. Do you think she'd be open to working with you? I've heard good things about her work.'

'She's extremely talented,' Finn said. 'How about I run it by her and let you know?'

'That would be great. Nice to talk to you, Finn.'

'You too.'

Finn clicked off his phone and looked at Tolstoy. 'Tell me I'm not an idiot for agreeing to work with Zoey on this account.'

The cat gave him a lugubrious stare.

Zoey decided to check in on her father on her way home from her dress fitting with Millie. Calling on him unannounced was always a little risky, not to mention stressful, but she was pleasantly surprised to find him in good spirits, and thankfully there was no obvious appearance that he'd been recently indulging in the alcoholic ones.

'Zoey, I was just about to call you. I have some good news.' He waved her inside, his face beaming.

She gave him the side-eye on the way in. 'Please don't tell me you're getting married again.'

'No, no, no.' He chuckled and closed the front door. 'It's way more exciting than that. I've sold the business. I got a takeover offer I couldn't refuse. I've just signed off on it.'

Zoey looked at him in shell-shocked silence, her thoughts flying off at tangents. *Sold?* How could the business be sold? She opened and closed her mouth, unable to find her voice for a moment. How could her father have done such a thing without even consulting her? Did she matter so little to him? Did he care nothing for her? She narrowed her eyes, her heart beating so heavily she could feel it pounding in her ears. 'What do you mean you've sold it? Are you sure you haven't been drinking?'

'Zoey.' His tone was that of an adult speaking to a cognitively dull child. 'I've only been drinking because of the stress of trying to run the business on my own. This will mean I can finally relax and—'

'But you wouldn't have had to run it on your own if you'd let me be a director!' She swung away with her hands clasped against her nose and mouth, trying to get her breathing under control.

How could this be happening? She had worked so damn hard. Covering for her father when he didn't meet a deadline. Filling in for him at meetings when he was nursing yet another hangover. She had compromised herself on so many occasions in an effort to keep the company's reputation intact. How could he go behind her back and sell the business without even talking it over with her first?

Zoey lowered her hands to stare at him with wild eyes. 'I can't believe you've done this. How could you…you betray me like this? You know how much the company means to me. Why didn't you discuss it with me? Why deliver it as a fait accompli?'

'Because I knew you would be against it, especially when you hear who's behind the takeover.'

Zoey stared at her father, her scalp prickling with unease. 'And are you going to tell me who this person is?'

'Finn O'Connell.'

'Finn O'Connell?' Zoey gasped. 'You can't be serious. Not him. Anyone but him.'

'I approached him and he jumped at the chance. He's had his eye on the company for a couple of months, asking me how things were going and so on. That's why I gave him first dibs.'

'A couple of months?' Zoey's voice came out as a shriek and her stomach churned fast enough to make butter. If what her father said was true, Finn had slept with her knowing he had his eye on her father's business. He had not said a word to her.

Not a single word.

Not even a hint.

Her father's betrayal suddenly didn't seem half as bad when she had Finn's duplicity to get her head around. Her hatred of him had gone on the back burner after their night of passion, in fact she had even wondered if it could be downgraded to mild dislike rather than pure unmitigated hatred.

But now her rage towards him was a tornado brewing in her body, making her physically shake with the effort to keep it under some semblance of control. Her head was pounding with tension, as if her temples were clamped in the cruel blunt jaws of a vice. She opened and closed her hands, her fingers feeling tingling and slightly numb, as if their blood supply had been cut off in the effort to keep her heart pumping. 'I—I can't believe that man would stoop so low.'

'Zoey, it's a business deal, there's nothing personal about it,' her father said in that same annoying 'adult to dull child' tone. 'Finn is keen to expand his business. He's done other highly successful takeovers. Anyway, I've lost the fire in my belly for the ad game. It's a perfect time for me to take early retirement, and you should be happy for me instead of harping on as if I've mortally wounded you.'

'You have mortally wounded me!' Zoey's voice rose in pitch, her eyes stinging with tears she refused to shed. She would *not* cry in front of her father. He would see it as a weakness and berate her for it, using her emotional response as yet another reason why he had sold the business out from under her. She took a couple of deep breaths and lowered her voice to a more reasonable level. 'What I'd like to know is, what happens to me? To my career?'

'You can work for Finn.'

Over my dead and rotting body. Zoey kept her

expression under tight control but her anger towards Finn was boiling inside her belly like a toxic brew. She had never loathed someone more than she did Finn O'Connell at that moment. And she couldn't wait to tell him so to his too-handsome face. 'That's not going to happen,' she said. 'Not unless he gives me an offer I can't refuse.'

But she would refuse it anyway on principle. She would beg on the streets before she would have Finn lauding it over her as her boss. Oh, God, her boss. Could there be a worse form of torture?

'If Finn O'Connell wants something badly enough, he doesn't mind paying top dollar for it.'

Zoey gave an evil gleam of a vengeful smile. 'Oh, he'll pay for it. I'll make damn sure of it.'

CHAPTER FIVE

ZOEY DECIDED AGAINST calling Finn because she had a burning desire to see him in person. What she had to say to him was not suitable for a phone conversation. She wanted to see every nuance on his face, read every flicker of his expression, to gain some insight into whether he felt compromised by what he had done. She suspected not, but she had to know for certain. The fact he'd slept with her whilst knowing he was in the process of taking over her father's business churned her gut.

Why, oh why, had she fallen for his practised charm? Could there be a more humiliating experience?

But when she got to his office the smartly dressed middle-aged woman at the reception desk informed her Finn was working at home that day.

'What's his address, then?' Zoey asked. 'I'll see him there.'

The woman gave Zoey an up and down, assessing look, her lips pursing in a disapproving manner. 'I'm afraid I can't give you that information. But, if you'd like to make an appointment, Mr O'Connell will see you when he's next available. However, it might not be for a week or two.' She gave a tight smile that didn't reach her eyes and added, 'As you can imagine, he's a very busy man.'

Zoey ground her teeth so hard she thought she'd be on a liquid diet for the next month. She drew in a breath, releasing it in a measured stream, and leaned her hands on the desk, nailing the other woman's gaze. 'Listen, there's no point looking at me like that. I already have his phone number. What I have to say to him needs to be said face to face.'

'Then why don't you just video call him?'

'And have him hang up on me? No way. I want to see him in person. Today. Within the next half hour, if possible. I don't care how busy he is, either in his private or professional life, but I am not leaving this office until you give me his address.'

The receptionist arched her brows, her posture as stiff and as unyielding as a bouncer at a nightclub. 'Your name is?'

Zoey straightened from the desk, furious she was being treated like one of Finn's love-struck bimbos. 'Zoey Brackenfield.'

The woman's expression underwent a rapid change, her haughtiness fading to be replaced by a look of delighted surprise. 'Oh, so *you're* Zoey Brackenfield.' She shot up from her ergonomic chair and held out her hand across the reception counter, a smile threatening to split her face in two. 'How lovely to meet you. I just adored the dog food commercial you did a while back. I started feeding my dog that brand because of you. It was just fabulous.'

'Thank you,' Zoey said, briefly shaking the woman's hand. But, compliments aside, she refused to back down and added in a pointed tone, 'His address?'

The woman shifted her lips from side to side, her eyes beginning to twinkle like fairy lights. 'I'd be happy to give it to you. No doubt you want to discuss the takeover.' She picked up a pen and wrote the address on a sticky note and handed it across the desk. 'It's about time Finn met his match.'

Zoey took the sticky note with a grim, no-teeth-showing smile. 'Oh, he's more than met his match.' And then she whipped round and left.

Finn lived in a leafy street in Chelsea in a gorgeous Georgian-style three-storey mansion. There was a small formal front garden with a neatly trimmed box hedge set behind a shiny, black wrought-iron fence. There were three colourful window boxes at the first-floor level, lush with vermillion pelargoniums and yellow-hearted purple pansies and trailing blue and white lobelia. But Zoey wasn't here to admire the view, even if part of her was as green as that box hedge with envy. If the outside visage was any measure, it was a dream of a house. What a pity such an arrogant jerk owned it.

Zoey pushed open the front gate and marched up the path to the front door and placed her finger on the brass doorbell button and left it there. She heard it echoing through the house and after a few moments the sound of firm footsteps from inside.

Finn answered the door with a welcoming smile. 'Ah, just who I was about to call. Come in.'

Zoey pushed past him, her chest heaving. She waited until he'd closed the door before she turned on him. 'You despicable, double-crossing jerk. How dare you buy—?'

'I take it you've heard about the takeover?' His expression was neutral, no sign of guilt, shame or conflict. Even his tone was irritatingly mild.

She clenched her hands into tight fists, her gaze blazing. 'I'm just dying to hear your explanation about why you didn't tell me you were taking over my father's company the night we…we…' She couldn't say the words without wanting to slap him.

'You've got it all wrong, babe. Your father approached me and offered to sell only a couple of days ago.'

Zoey stood rigidly before him, her blood boiling. How could she believe him? Why should she believe him? 'Did you do it deliberately? The whole laptop switch thing, the one-nighter, the secret takeover...was it all just a game to you? Was *I* just a silly little game to you?'

A muscle in Finn's jaw flickered just the once, as if he was holding back a retort. He let out a slow breath and made a placating gesture with one of his hands. 'Look, nothing was deliberate, other than I agreed to buy your father out when he came to me the other day. I couldn't tell you about the takeover because he didn't want me to. He insisted on absolute secrecy or the deal was off. If you want to be angry with anyone, it should be him.'

'I am angry with him!' Zoey said. 'But I'm even more furious with you. You should have given me the heads up. I had a right to know.'

'That's not the way I do business,' Finn said with annoying calm. 'Your father wanted to keep it under wraps and, while I didn't necessarily agree with it, I respected his decision. Besides, you supposedly hate my guts, so why would I jeopardise the takeover by letting you in on it? You might have leaked it to someone to stop me from—'

'When did he approach you? Before or after we...we...had sex?'

'After.'

Zoey wasn't quite ready to believe him even

though she found, somewhat to her surprise, that she desperately wanted to. 'But he said you'd had an eye on the company for a couple of months.'

'I'm interested in all of my competitors,' Finn said. 'I've run into your father a few times over the last couple of months and we talked shop, but I did not at any time make him an offer. He came to my office a couple of days after we got back from New York.'

'So…so why did you sleep with me?'

'I slept with you because it was what we both wanted.' His eyes contained a dark glitter that sent a shiver skating down her spine. 'And I would hazard a guess and say you want to do it again.'

Zoey coughed out a disdainful laugh. 'You're freaking unbelievable. Your ego is so big it deserves its own zip code. Its own government.' She jabbed her index finger into his rock-hard chest. 'You disgust me.' Jab. 'I hate you more than anyone I know.' Jab. Jab. 'You played me right from the start.' Jab. Jab. Jab. 'But I won't let you—'

'What?' He grabbed her hand before she could aim another jab at his chest. 'Tempt you into bed again? You want me just as much as I want you. That night was something out of the ordinary for both of us. That's why you're here now instead of calling me on the phone to tear strips off me. What you want to tear off me is my clothes. You couldn't keep yourself away, could you, babe?'

Zoey tried to pull out of his hold but his grip tightened and a tingling sensation ran down the backs of her legs like a flock of scurrying insects. Not fear, not panic but lust. And how she hated herself for it. 'Let go of me before I slap your arrogant face.'

Finn tugged her closer, his gaze holding hers in a smouldering lock that sent another shiver scuttling down the backs of her legs. 'I'm not averse to a bit of edgy sex now and again but I draw the line at violence.' He placed his other hand in the small of her back, bringing her flush against him, allowing her to feel the potency of his arousal. And she almost melted into a liquid pool of longing right there and then. 'So, how about we make love not war, hmm?'

Zoey watched as his mouth came down, as if in slow motion, but she didn't do anything to resist. She couldn't. She was transfixed by the throbbing energy between their hard-pressed bodies. His body was calling out to hers in a language older than time. The language of lust—full-blooded, primal lust that craved only one outcome.

His lips met hers and something wild and feral was unleashed inside her. She opened her lips to the bold thrust of his tongue, welcoming him in, swept up in the scorching moment of madness, driven by desire so scorching it was threatening to blister her skin inside and out. Her lips clung to his, her free hand grasping the front of his shirt, her lower body on fire. Giant leaping flames of fire raged throughout her pelvis.

Never had she wanted a man like this one. He incited in her the most out of control urges, turning her into someone she didn't recognise. He turned her into a wanton woman who didn't care about anything but assuaging the raging desire overtaking her body. She fed off his mouth, her tongue playing with his in a catch-me-if-you-can caper, then sent another wave of heat through her female flesh. Her inner core flickered with sensations, hungry, pulsing sensations that built to a pulsating crescendo.

Finn released her other hand, winding both his arms around her, one of his hands going to the curve of her bottom, pushing her harder into his erection. 'No one drives me as wild with lust as you. No one.'

'I'm not sleeping with you again,' Zoey said breathlessly against his mouth. *But I want to so much!* Every cell in her body wanted him. Every pounding beat of her heart echoed with the need for more of his touch. Every inch of her flesh was vibrating with longing. Intoxicating, torturous longing.

'Who said anything about sleeping?' His mouth came back down firmly, desperately, drawing from her an even more fervent response.

Zoey placed her hands in his hair, tugging and releasing the thick black strands, relishing the sounds of his guttural groans as he deepened the kiss even further. One of Finn's hands moved up under her top, cupping her bra-clad breast, his thumb rolling over the already tightly budded nipple. Tingling sensations rippled through her flesh, the covering of lace no match for the incendiary heat and fire of his touch.

But somehow through the enveloping fog of desire a tiny beam of reality shone through. She was falling under his spell again, melting like tallow in his arms, and she had to put a stop to it while she still could. If she still could. Her pride depended on it.

Zoey pulled out of his hold and swiped a hand across her mouth as if to remove the taste of him from her lips. 'No. This can't happen. Not again.'

Finn shrugged as if it didn't matter either way and that made her hate him all the more. How dared he not be as affected by their kiss as her? Her whole body was quivering with need. A pounding need that threatened to overrule her self-control. 'Fine. Your call.'

Zoey stepped a couple of paces away, wrapping her arms around her still throbbing body. 'You must be out of your mind to think I would sleep with you again after what you've done.'

'All I've done is buy a company that was in

danger of falling over,' Finn said. 'You know it's true, Zoey. Your father isn't capable of running the business any more. He's burnt out and ready to retire and he can do it more than comfortably with the price I paid to buy him out.'

'But *I'm* capable of running it,' she shot back. 'He had no right to sell it to you without even discussing it with me.'

'That's something you'll have to settle with him. But you and I have other business to discuss first.' He gestured to a sitting room off the large foyer. 'Come this way.'

Zoey wanted to refuse but something about his expression told her it would be wise to stay and hear him out. Besides, her job was on the line. She had to know what her options were, if there *were* options available to her. But her mind was reeling so badly with shock, anger and bitter disappointment she couldn't think clearly.

What would happen to her career now? She had pictured a long, productive career at Brackenfield Advertising, hopefully one day taking over as director. Proving to her father—and, yes, even proving to herself—she had the ability, drive and talent to do it.

But it had all been ripped out from under her.

All her plans, her hopes, her dreams and aspirations were hanging in the balance.

Zoey followed Finn down the long, wide hall

into a beautifully decorated sitting room off the spacious hall. The polished timber floor was covered by a huge Persian rug that only left about a foot of the floorboards showing around the edges of the room. She stood for a moment, struck by the décor, the luxury carpet threatening to swallow her up to the ankles.

There was a fireplace with a marble mantelpiece above and two luxurious white sofas and a wing chair upholstered in a finely checked fabric for contrast. Various works of art hung on the walls—most of them looked like originals—and the central light above was a crystal chandelier with matching wall lights positioned at various points around the room to provide a more muted lighting effect.

The room overlooked a stunning, completely private back garden with espaliered pear trees along the stone boundary wall. Neatly trimmed, low border hedges ran either side of the flagstone pathway, which led to an outdoor eating area, the light-coloured wrought-iron setting in the French provincial style. No expense had been spared in making the property a showpiece. It was stylish, ultra-luxurious and commodious. The sitting room alone could have swallowed up half of her flat and left room to spare.

It occurred to Zoey that if she didn't keep her job in some form or the other she wouldn't have enough to pay her rent in the long term. Without Ivy and Millie chipping in now they had both moved out, it made for a very tight budget indeed. She would be able to manage for a few months, quite a few months, but what then? How long could she expect to survive? She certainly wasn't going to ask her father for any hand-outs, nor bunk down at his house. She would rather sleep under a sheet of cardboard on the streets.

Finn walked over to a cleverly concealed bar fridge in a cabinet below a wall of bookshelves. 'Would you like a drink?'

Zoey stood at some distance, not trusting herself to be any closer to him. 'A brandy—make it a double. I have a feeling I'm not going to like what you've got to say.'

'Now now, there's no need to be so dramatic,' he chided gently. 'You might be pleasantly surprised in what I have to tell you.' He poured two snifters of brandy into two ball-shaped glasses and then came over to her to hand her one. 'There you go.'

Zoey took the glass but wasn't able to avoid touching his fingers as she did so. The lightning bolt of sensual energy shot up her arm and went straight to a fizzing inferno in her core. Every moment of their scorching night of passion rushed back to her in a flash, as if her skin would never forget the intoxicating intensity of his touch. It was burned, branded into her flesh, and she would never forget it and never become impervious to it. How could the merest brush of his fingers cause such an eruption of longing? She took a large sip of brandy, but it burned her throat, and she began to cough and splutter.

Finn took the glass back from her and patted her on the back. 'Whoa, there. Better take it a little more slowly.'

Zoey shrugged off his hand and glowered at him, her cheeks on fire. 'I want to know what you plan to do with the staff, myself included.'

He idly swirled the contents of his glass, his gaze watching the whirlpool he created in a calm fashion before his gaze fixed back on hers. 'There will, of course, be some trimming—'

'And no doubt I'll be the first to go.'

He held her glare with the same implacable calm, his eyes giving nothing away. 'That will depend.'

Zoey narrowed her eyes to paper-thin slits. 'On what?' Whether she had a fling with him? Was he going to hold her to ransom, offering to keep her on the staff if she gave him access to her body? If so, he had another think coming. And, frankly, so did her body, which was already threatening to betray her and jump at the chance of another night in his arms.

One side of his mouth tilted in a sardonic smile, a knowing glint reflected in his eyes. 'Not on that.'

Zoey suppressed a shiver. 'I don't believe you.'

'I may be a little ruthless at times, but blackmail isn't my style.'

He probably didn't have to resort to blackmail since he only had to crook his little finger and women would flock to him. And Zoey had to be careful she didn't join them, which would have been a whole lot easier if he wasn't so impossibly, irresistibly attractive. She kept her gaze trained on his. 'At the risk of repeating myself, I don't believe you.'

Finn put his brandy glass down, as if he had lost interest in it. He met her gaze with his now inscrutable one. 'I had a call from Leo Frascatelli this afternoon.'

Zoey's heart sank like an anchor. Not just any old anchor—a battleship's anchor. She had lost the contract. Lost it to Finn O'Connell. Oh God, could her circumstances get any more humiliating? He had taken everything from her—her father's business, her career hopes and dreams and the Frascatelli contract. If it wasn't bad enough Finn had bought Brackenfield Advertising out from under her, now she would have to stomach his gloating over winning the account she had hoped would be hers.

She threw him a livid glare, her top lip curling. 'Congratulations. Who did you sleep with to nail that little prize?'

One side of his mouth curved upwards in a half-smile, his dark eyes shining with a mysterious light. 'No one. I was just about to call you about the call from Leo before you showed up on my doorstep in a towering rage.'

'Spare me the brag-fest or I might vomit on your nice cream carpet.'

'It would be no more than Tolstoy has done in the past.'

Zoey frowned. 'Tolstoy?'

As if he had heard his name mentioned, a Russian blue cat with only one eye came strolling into the room, the tinkling of his collar bell overly loud in the silence. The cat completely ignored Finn and came padding over to Zoey, winding around her ankles and bumping its head against her with a mewling sound.

'Zoey, allow me to introduce you to Tolstoy,' Finn said.

Zoey bent down to stroke the cat's head. 'Oh, you darling thing. But you look like you've been in the wars.' Tolstoy purred like a train and bumped his head against her petting hand. 'Aren't you a friendly boy, hey?'

'You have the magic touch, it seems,' Finn said. 'He normally hates strangers. He usually runs away and hides, or worse, attacks them.'

Yes, well, look who was talking about having the magic touch. Zoey was still tingling from head to foot from Finn's heart-stopping kiss. She straightened from petting the cat and met Finn's unreadable gaze. 'How long have you had him?'

'Five months. I found him injured on my way home one night and took him to a vet. They traced the owner via the microchip, but they no longer wanted him. So, I took him in. And paid the eye-watering vet bills.'

'Oh…that was…nice of you.'

Finn's mouth flickered with a wry smile. 'You sound surprised that I can be nice on occasion.'

Zoey elevated her chin. 'I'm sure you can lay on the charm when you want things to go your way. But just for the record—it won't work with me.'

Finn waved to the sofa nearest her, his lips twitching and his eyes twinkling. 'Take a seat. I haven't finished telling you the good news about the Frascatelli account.'

Zoey sat on the sofa and some of the tension in her body dissipated as the deep feather cushioning dipped to take her weight. Tolstoy jumped up beside her, nudging her hand to get her to continue petting him. She absently stroked the cat, but she fought against the temptation to relax. She was in enemy territory and she had to avoid a repeat of what happened between her and Finn the other night.

Anyway, what good news could there be? She had lost the account to Finn. But why had he found out first and she had not even been told her pitch had been unsuccessful? 'Are you friends with Leonardo Frascatelli?' she asked, eyeing him suspiciously.

Finn sat on the opposite sofa, one arm resting on the arm rest. He hitched one leg over the other, resting his ankle on his bent knee in a relaxed pose. His gaze wandered to the cat she was stroking beside her and a flicker of a wry smile passed across his lips. 'We're casual acquaintances but he is too much of a professional to allow any nepotism to influence his decision. He couldn't decide between your pitch and mine, so he's asked both of us to do it. How do you feel about working with me on the account?'

Zoey stared at him in numb shock, a combination of dread and excitement stirring in her blood. 'You mean we *both* won it?' Her voice came out like a squeak and Tolstoy suddenly started and jumped off the sofa. And, twitching his tail, he stalked out of the room with an air of affronted dignity.

'Yep, and he asked me to run it by you first to see if you're willing to share the contract with me,' Finn said. 'It'll mean working together a fair bit but I'm game if you are.' The enigmatic light in his eyes played havoc with her already on-edge nerves. What would 'working with him' entail?

Zoey moistened her paper-dry lips, her heart

kicking against her breastbone at the thought of being in Finn O'Connell's company for extended periods. Could she do it? Could she take on this project—this enormously lucrative project—and come out the other side with her pride intact?

'I—I'm having trouble understanding how this will work. I mean, you now apparently own Brackenfield Advertising. Am I going to be working under the Brackenfield banner or—?'

'The Brackenfield banner will no longer exist.' His tone was brutally blunt. 'I want you to work for me. The Frascatelli account can be your trial period. If all goes well, you can stay on with me. But if you'd like to explore other options, then that's fine too. It's up to you.'

Zoey sprang off the sofa and began to pace the floor in agitation. Brackenfield Advertising would no longer exist? Her job, her future, her career path was now under Finn O'Connell's control. Could there be anything more galling than to be totally under his command and authority? She spun round to face him, her chest pounding with rage. 'I didn't think it was possible to hate someone as much as I hate you. You've taken my future from me. You've stolen my father's company from me and—'

'I paid well above what I should have for your father's business,' Finn said, rising from the sofa with indolent ease. 'It's not been firing at peak performance for months and you damn well know it.'

'I've done my best, but my father wouldn't make me a director, so I was completely hamstrung,' Zoey fired back. 'Plus, I was always covering for him when he missed a deadline or failed to show up at a meeting. But I had it under control. I was bringing in a more or less steady stream of work and—'

'Look, all credit to you for caring about your father, but you're not helping him by covering for him all the time,' Finn said. 'He needs to face his demons and get some help before it's too late. And you're currently in the way of him getting that help.'

On one level, Zoey knew what he said had an element of truth to it. But she hated him too much to give him the satisfaction of telling him so. She thrust her hands on her hips and upped her chin, her eyes throwing sparks of ire at him.

'What would you know about my situation? You with your mouth full of silver spoons and oozing with privilege! You haven't any idea of the struggle it is to keep someone you love from making a complete ass of themselves.'

Something flickered over his face, a quiver of inner conflict at the back of his eyes. 'I know more about that than you probably realise.' His voice contained an odd note she had never heard him use before. A disquieting note, a chord of emotional pain buried so deep inside you could only hear its faint echo ringing in the silence.

Zoey opened her mouth but then closed it again when he turned to pick up his brandy glass from where he had left it. He studied the contents of the glass for a moment, then gave her a sideways glance. 'You speak of my privilege? There are no privileges, no silver spoons, when your parents drink and smoke every penny that comes in the door.'

He gave a grim smile and continued, holding the glass up. 'See this? One drink was never enough for either of my parents. If they had one, they had to have twenty.' He put the glass down with a dull thud. 'And don't get me started on the drugs.'

Zoey swallowed a tight stricture in her throat, ashamed of herself for making assumptions about his background. From what he had said so far, *she* was the one who had grown up with the silver spoons and privilege. 'I'm sorry. I didn't realise things were like that for you…'

Finn turned to put the glass of brandy down again, his expression becoming masked, as if talking about the past was something he found imminently distasteful. 'I'll give you five days to decide what you want to do regarding the Frascatelli project.'

His manner and tone had switched to brisk and businesslike efficiency with such speed, Zoey was a little slow to keep up. She was still musing over his disadvantaged childhood, marvelling at how he had built an advertising empire that was one of the most successful in the world. An empire she was being invited to join…if she could stomach working with him on the Frascatelli project first.

But how could she refuse? It was a project she had dreamed of working on ever since she'd first heard about it. She would have to keep strict boundaries around their working relationship. There could be no repeats of the other night. And her self-control would have to go to boot camp to get back in shape for the months ahead. Finn O'Connell was known to be a demanding boss, but a generous one.

Besides that, she needed a job.

'I'll give my answer now, if you don't mind.'

Finn held her gaze for a long beat, nothing in his expression suggesting he cared either way what her decision was. Zoey drew in a quick breath and released it in a single stream. 'I accept your offer. However, there are some rules I'd like to stipulate first.'

A marble-hard look came into his eyes and the base of her spine tingled. 'Come and see me in my office first thing tomorrow and we'll talk some more. But just to give you the heads up—I'm the one who makes the rules.'

'But I want to talk to you now.'

'Not now.' There was a note of intransigence in his tone and he pushed back his shirt cuff and gave his watch a pointed glance before adding, 'I have to be somewhere soon.'

Zoey gave him an arch look. 'A hot little hook-up waiting for you, is there?'

His unreadable eyes flicked to her mouth for a heart-stopping moment before reconnecting with her gaze. 'Tomorrow, nine a.m. sharp.' He gave a dismissive on-off smile and led the way to the door. 'I'll see you out in case you can't find your way.'

Zoey brushed past him. 'Don't bother. I can find my own way out.' And she marched out of the room, down the hall and out of the front door, giving it a satisfying slam on her exit.

Finn released a long breath and scraped a hand through his hair. He wasn't sure what had led him to reveal to Zoey the shabby little secrets of his parents' life choices. It wasn't something he bandied about to all and sundry. Everyone had a right to a little privacy, and he guarded that aspect of his life with religious zeal. He had spent too many years of his childhood wishing his parents were different. And, as Zoey did with her father, he too had enabled his parents at times in a bid to keep some semblance of normal family life together.

But it had backfired on him time and time again. His parents were addicts and they had only ever fleetingly taken responsibility for their cravings. A week or two here and there, a month, once even three months of being sober, but then they would drift back into their habits and he would be shipped off to relatives again. In the end, he had drawn a line in the sand and told them straight out—get clean or get out of his life. They'd chosen to get out of his life.

Tolstoy peered round the corner of the sitting room, his one-eyed stare wary. Finn bent down and scooped the cat up before it could turn its back on him. 'You're a traitor, do you hear me?' He stroked the soft fur of the cat's head and was rewarded with a rhythmic purr. 'But she is rather irresistible, isn't she?'

The cat nudged his hand and purred some more. Finn gave a crooked smile and continued stroking him. 'I'm glad you've forgiven me but I'm not sure if Zoey's going to.' He set the cat back down on the floor and Tolstoy sat and gave one of those gymnastically complicated leg-in-the-air licks of his nether regions.

Finn had all along considered Zoey's position when it had come to the takeover of her father's company, but he was a man of his word, and since Harry Brackenfield had insisted on secrecy that was what Finn had adhered to. There was a part of him that completely understood her angst and disappointment. Besides, didn't he know all about having your heart set on something only for it to be ripped away? But business was business and he didn't allow emotion to muddy the waters. He wanted to expand his own company and taking the best people from Brackenfield was a sure way to do it.

And Zoey was high on that list.

Finn had cut short his time with Zoey just now, not because he wanted to but because he needed to. There was only so much he was willing to reveal about his background and he was surprised he had revealed as much as he had. He wasn't used to letting people in to the darker aspects of his life. He didn't get close enough to people to share things he wished he could forget. There was no point revisiting the train wreck of his childhood. It never changed anything other than to make him feel even more bitter about his parents' lack of love and care for his well-being.

It was one of the reasons he had ruled out having a family of his own. Not because he didn't think he would do a good job as a father—after all, it wouldn't be too difficult to lift a little higher than the abysmal benchmark his father had set—but because he genuinely didn't want anyone needing him, relying on him, expecting him to be someone he knew he couldn't be. He didn't have the emotional repertoire for such a long-haul commitment. He was too ruthless, too driven, too independent and too self-sufficient.

He enjoyed being a free agent. He had never desired a long-term partner. The thought of developing lasting feelings for someone made him uneasy. Loving someone who didn't or couldn't love you back was too terrifying. He had been there as a child and never wanted to experience that sinking sense of loss again. He found that, within a week or two of being with someone, he began looking for a way out once the thrilling, blood-pumping chase was over. Time to move on to more exciting ventures.

But somehow, with Zoey, Finn sensed a different dynamic going on between them. She excited him in ways no one else had managed to do. Her stubborn prickliness both amused and frustrated him, and her feistiness was the biggest turn-on he had experienced. She was whip-smart and sharp-tongued and sensationally sexy, and he knew working with her was going to be one of the most exciting periods in his life. He didn't normally mix business with pleasure—the pitfalls were well-documented—but this time he was making an exception for an exceptional woman.

And he couldn't wait to start.

CHAPTER SIX

ZOEY ARRIVED AT Finn's office the following morning right on the stroke of nine a.m. She had spent a restless night ruminating over her situation, agonising over whether she was being a fool for agreeing to work with him. It would mean close contact, hours of close contact, and who knew what such proximity would produce? Another firestorm of lust? It must not happen. She must not give in to temptation. She must not be hoodwinked by Finn's charm and allure.

She. Must. Not.

Finn's middle-aged receptionist-cum-secretary smiled as Zoey came through the door. 'Good morning, Ms Brackenfield. Finn will be here shortly—something must have held him up. He's normally bang on time. Can I get you a coffee while you wait?'

Something had held him up, had it? Like a sleepover with one of his avid fans? Zoey painted a polite smile on her face while inside she was seething. No doubt some other foolish young woman had capitulated to his practised charm. No way was Zoey going to fall for it a second time—even if it had been the most spectacular sex of her entire life. 'No, thank you. Erm...please call me Zoey. Sorry, but I didn't catch your name the last time.'

'June,' the older woman said with a smile. 'Congratulations on the Frascatelli account. Finn told me you'll be sharing the contract with him. Are you excited?'

A part of Zoey was far more excited than she had any business being, but not just about the Frascatelli contract. The traitorous part of her that couldn't think of her night of passion with Finn without a frisson going through her body. The wild and reckless part of her that still smouldered and simmered with longing. 'I'm sure it will be an interesting experience,' she said, keeping her expression under tight control.

June's eyes danced. 'I'm sure you'll get on together famously.' She glanced behind Zoey's shoulder to the front entrance and added, 'Ah, here he is now.'

Zoey turned to see Finn striding through the door looking remarkably refreshed and heart-stoppingly handsome as usual. He obviously hadn't spent a sleepless night ruminating over what lay ahead. He had probably bedded some young nubile woman and had bed-wrecking sex while Zoey had spent the evening in a state of sexual frustration. One taste of him and she was addicted. How did it happen?

And how on God's sweet earth was she to control it?

He was wearing a charcoal-grey suit with an open-necked white shirt and looked every inch the suave man about town who didn't have a care in the world. Or did he? His revelation about his less than perfect childhood had totally stunned her. Never would she have envisaged him as the product of disadvantage. He had made such a success of his company, he had wealth beyond most people's wildest dreams and he had no shortage of female attention—hers included.

If only she could turn off this wretched attraction to him. If anything, it was getting worse, not better.

'Morning,' Finn said, encompassing both his receptionist and Zoey with a smile. 'Come this way, Zoey.' He glanced back at June and added, 'Hold my calls, June. And can you reschedule tonight's meeting with Peter Greenbaum? Zoey and I are having dinner instead.'

Dinner? Zoey ground her teeth behind her impassive expression. The arrogance of the man. He hadn't even asked her.

'Will do,' June said, reaching for the phone.

Zoey waited until she was alone with Finn in his office before she took him to task. She gave him an arch look. 'Dinner? Funny, but I don't recall you asking me to dinner.'

'I didn't ask.' He flicked her a glance on his way to his desk. 'But I'm telling you now. Take a seat.'

Zoey stayed exactly where she was. 'I'm not going to be ordered about by you. I have other plans for this evening.'

He shrugged off his jacket and hung it in a slimline cupboard against the wall. Then he came and stood behind his desk with his hands resting on the back of his ergonomic chair, a flinty look in his eyes. 'Cancel them. We have work to do.'

She folded her arms across her middle. 'Work? Are you sure that's what's on the agenda?'

His eyes drifted to her mouth and then back to her eyes, an indolent smile lifting up one side of his mouth. 'Work is on my agenda but who knows what's on yours?'

Zoey wasn't one to blush easily, but she could feel heat pouring into her cheeks. She lifted her chin and glued her gaze to his, determined not to be the first to look away. 'Before we begin working together, I think we need to set some ground rules.'

He rolled back his chair and sat down, leaned back and made a steeple with his fingers in front of his chest, his gaze unwavering on hers. 'I told you last night, I'm the one who makes the rules. You get to follow them.'

Zoey came over to stand in front of his desk and, leaning her hands on it, nailed him with a steely glare. 'Let me get something straight—I will *not* be ordered around by you.'

He slowly rocked his chair from side to side, his fingers still steepled in front of his chest. And, judging from his expression, he was seemingly unmoved by her curt statement. 'If you can't follow simple instructions then you won't have a future working for me once we finish this project.'

Zoey pushed herself away from his desk with an unladylike curse. 'Why do I get the feeling you only bought Brackenfield Advertising to have me under your control?'

He raised one dark eyebrow. 'My, oh my, what a vivid imagination you have.' He released his steepled fingers and leaned forward to rest his forearms on the desk. 'I told you why I bought it. It was about to go under. I was doing your dad a favour. And you too, when it comes to that.'

'I'm surprised you wanted to help him given he's nothing but a rotten drunk like your parents.'

The ensuing silence was so thick and palpable Zoey could feel it pressing on her from all four corners of the room. Nothing showed in Finn's expression that her words had upset him in any way, yet she got the sense that behind the screen of his eyes it was a different story. Shame coursed through her at her uncharitable outburst. She knew nothing of his parents' issues other than the small amount he had told her. And, given her own issues with her father, she understood all too well how heartbreaking it was to see a parent self-destruct, and feeling so useless to do anything to prevent it.

'I—I'm sorry,' Zoey said. 'That was completely uncalled for.'

Finn lifted his forearms off the desk and leaned back in his chair. 'What I told you last night was in confidence. Understood?'

She couldn't hold his gaze and lowered it to stare at the paperweight on his desk. 'Understood.' She bit down into her lower lip, wanting to inflict physical pain on herself for being so unnecessarily cruel.

Finn pushed back his chair and went over to the window overlooking a spectacular view of the Thames and Tower Bridge. He stood with his back to her for a moment or two, his hands thrust into his trouser pockets, the tension in his back and shoulders clearly visible through the fine cotton of his shirt.

He finally released a heavy-sounding breath and turned back to face her, his expression shadowed by the light coming in from the window now behind him. 'I probably don't need to tell you how hard it is to see your parents make a train wreck of their lives.'

'No...you don't.'

He took his hands out of his pockets and sent one through the thickness of his hair, the line of his mouth grim. 'My parents were hippies, flower children who suddenly found themselves the parents of a baby they hadn't planned on having, or at least not at that stage of their lives. They were barely out of their teens and had nothing behind them. So, when it all got too much, they drank or smoked dope to cope.'

He screwed up his mouth into a grimace. 'One of my first memories was trying to wake them both so I could have something to eat and drink. I think I was only three. It took me a long while—ten years, actually—until I realised they were completely unreliable. I gave them a couple of chances to lift their game but of course, they couldn't live without their addictions. So, I finally drew a line in the sand when I was thirteen and gave them a choice. It was no big surprise they chose the drink and drugs.'

Zoey's heart contracted at the neglect he had suffered, and another wave of shame coursed through her for being so mean. How awful for such a small child to witness his care-givers acting so irresponsibly. How frightening it must have been for him to not be sure if he was going to get fed each day. 'I'm so sorry… I can't imagine how tough that must have been for you. To not feel safe with your own parents. To not know if you're even going to be fed and taken care of properly. How on earth did you survive it?'

Finn made a gruff sound in the back of his throat. 'I was farmed out to distant relatives from time to time. I would go back to my parents when they dried out for a bit and then the cycle would start all over again. By the time I got to my teens, I knew I would have to rely on myself and no one else to make something of my life. I studied hard, got a couple of part-time jobs, won a scholarship to a good school and the rest, as they say, is history.'

Zoey found herself standing in front of him without any clear memory of how she'd got there. But something in her compelled her to touch him, to reach out to him to show that she of all people understood some of what he had experienced. She placed her hand on his strong forearm, her fingers resting against hard male muscles, and a flicker of molten heat travelled in lightning-fast speed to her core.

'Finn…' Her voice got caught on something in her throat and she looked up into his dark brown eyes and tried again. 'I'm so ashamed of how I spoke to you. I admire you for overcoming such impossible odds to be where you are today. It's just amazing that you didn't let such an awful start in life ruin your own potential.'

His hand came down over hers and gave it a light squeeze, his eyes holding hers. 'For years, I did what you do for your father. I filled the gaps for them, compensated for them, made excuses for them. I just wanted a normal family and was prepared to go to extraordinary lengths to get it. But it was magical thinking. Some people aren't capable of changing, no matter how many chances you give them, so why wait around hoping one day they will?'

Zoey glanced at his hand covering hers and a faint shiver passed through her body. His touch on her body was a flame to bone-dry tinder. She could feel the nerves of her skin responding to him, the tingles, the quivers, the spreading warmth. She brought her gaze back to his to find him looking at her with dark intensity, his eyes moving between hers then dipping to her mouth.

The air seemed suddenly charged with a new energy, a vibrating energy she could feel echoing in the lower region of her body. A pulse, a drum-beat, a blood-driven throb.

She hitched in a breath and went to pull out of his light hold but he placed his other hand on the top of her shoulder, anchoring her gently in place. Anchoring her to him as surely as if she had been nailed to the floor. 'Finn…' Her voice came out in a barely audible whisper, her heart picking up its pace.

Finn's hand moved from her shoulder to cradle one side of her face, his thumb moving like a slow metronome arm across her cheek. Back and forth. Back and forth. A rhythmic, mesmerising beat. 'I'm guessing this is not part of your list of rules?' His voice was low and deep and husky, his eyes dark and glinting.

Zoe moistened her lips, knowing full well it was a tell-tale signal of wanting to be kissed but doing it anyway. Her eyes drifted to his mouth and a wave of heat flooded her being. 'That depends on what you're going to do.'

He tilted her face up so her eyes were in line with his. 'What do you think I'm going to do?'

'Kiss me.'

'Is that a request or a statement?'

Zoey stepped up on tiptoe and planted her hands on his broad chest, her fingers clutching at his shirt. 'It's a command,' she said, just within a hair's breadth of his lips.

Finn brought his mouth down on hers with a smothered groan, his other arm going around her back like an iron band. Her body erupted in a shower of tingles as she came into contact with his rock-hard frame, every cell throbbing with anticipation. His lips moved with increasing urgency against hers, his tongue driving through the seam of her lips with ruthless determination.

Zoey welcomed him in with her own groan of delight, her tongue playing with his in a sexy tango that sent her blood thundering through the network of her veins. The scrape of his rough skin against the smoothness of hers sent a frisson through her body, the erotic flicker of his tongue sending a lightning bolt of lust straight to her core. Molten heat flooded her system. Desire—hot, thick, dark desire—raced through her female flesh and drove every thought out of her mind but the task of satisfying the burning ache of need.

How had she thought one night of passion was ever going to be enough? It wasn't. It couldn't be. She needed him like she needed air. Needed to feel the explosive energy they created together, to make sure she hadn't imagined it the first time. It didn't mean she was having a fling with him, it didn't mean she was like one of his gushing fans—it meant she was a woman with needs who wanted them satisfied by a man who desired her as much as she desired him.

And what fervent desire it was, firing back and forth between their bodies like high-voltage electricity.

Finn walked her backwards to his desk, bending her back over it, ruthlessly scattering pens and sticky-note pads out of the way. He stepped between her legs, his expression alive with intent, and she shuddered in anticipation. 'If this is on your rules list then you'd better say so now before it's too late.'

'It's not… Oh, God, it's not…' Zoey could barely get her voice to work, so caught up was she in the heart-stopping moment. She wrapped her thighs hard around his body, her inner core pulsating with wet, primal need.

He leaned over her, one of his hands anchored to the desk, the other tugging her blouse out of her skirt to access her breast through her balcony bra. There was just enough of the upper curve of her breast outside the cup of lace for his mouth to explore. But soon it wasn't enough for him and he tugged the bra out of the way so his lips and tongue could wreak further havoc on her senses.

Zoey writhed with building pleasure on his desk, a part of her mind drifting above her body to look down on the spine-tingling tableau below. It was like an X-rated fantasy to have Finn feasting on her body in such an unbridled way. But in a way he *was* a fantasy. He wasn't the type of man she could see a future with, even if she was interested in a future with a man. He was too much of a playboy, too much of a charmer, for her to want to be with him any length of time.

But she wanted this. Wanted him with a burning, aching need that was beyond anything she had felt before. It pounded through her body, hammered in her blood, throbbed between her legs.

'I haven't been able to stop thinking about this since the last time we were together,' he said, kissing his way down her abdomen. 'Tell me to stop if you don't want me to go any further.'

Stop? No way was she letting him stop. Not while her body was quivering with longing, aching with the need to find release. 'Please don't stop…' Her voice was breathless, her spine arching off the desk as his hand drew up her skirt to bunch around her waist. 'Please don't stop or I'll kill you.'

A lazy smile backlit his gaze with a smouldering heat. 'Then, in the interests of occupational health and safety, I'd better do as you command.' He brought his mouth down to her mound, his fingers moving aside her knickers, his warm breath wafting against her sensitised flesh in a teasing breeze. 'So beautiful…' His voice was so low and deep, it sounded as if it came from beneath the floorboards.

His lips moved against her feminine folds, soft little touches that sent her pulse rate soaring. Shivers coursed down her legs and arms, flickers of molten heat deep in her core. He caressed her with his tongue, the slow strokes a form of exquisite torture, ramping up the pressure in her tender tissues until it was impossible to hold back the tumultuous wave. It crashed through her body as if a hurricane were powering it, booming, crashing waves that sent every thought out of her brain short of losing consciousness.

She bit back the urge to cry out, vaguely recalling Finn's receptionist was only a few metres away on the other side of the office door. Zoey was reduced to the pulsing pleasure of her primal body, transported to a place where only bliss could reside. The aftershocks kept coming, gradually subsiding to a gentle rocking through her flesh like the lap of idle waves on the shore.

Finn straightened her clothes into some sort of order, his expression one of glinting triumph. 'That was certainly a great way to start the day.' He held out his hand to help her up off the desk.

Zoey took his hand, her cheeks feeling as if they could cook a round of toast. She slipped down off his desk but grasped the front of his shirt. 'Not so fast, buddy. I haven't finished with you yet.'

Something dark and hot flared in the backs of his eyes. 'Now you've got my attention.'

Zoey pushed him back against the desk, stepping between his legs as he had done with her moments earlier. 'Lie down,' she commanded like a dominatrix, goaded on by the dark, sensual energy throbbing in her body—the same dark, sensual energy she could see reflected in his gaze.

Finn stood with his buttocks pressed against

the desk, his hands going to her upper arms. 'You don't have to do this.'

Zoey planted a firm hand on the middle of his chest. 'I said, lie down.'

He gave an indolent smile, his eyes holding hers in a spine-tingling lock. 'Make me.'

Zoey kept her gaze trained on his and reached for his zipper, sliding it down, down, down, watching the flicker of anticipation in his eyes, feeling the shudder that rippled through him against the press of her hand. 'Here's one of my rules. You don't get to pleasure me unless I can return the favour. Got it?'

Finn gave another whole-body shudder, his eyes dark and as lustrous as wet paint. 'Got it.'

'Good.' Zoey pushed him down so his back and shoulders were on the desk, his strongly muscled thighs either side of hers. She freed him from his underwear and bent her head to take him in her mouth, teasing him at first with soft little flicks of her tongue against his engorged flesh. He groaned and muttered a curse, his body quaking as she subjected him to her wildest fantasy.

She stroked her tongue down his turgid length, then circled the head of his erection, round and round and round, until he muttered another curse. Then she took him fully in her mouth, sucking on him deeply, not letting up until he finally capitulated in a powerful release that rattled every object still sitting on his desk. It thrilled her to the core of her being to have him prostrated before her with the same blood-pounding pleasure he had given her.

Zoey stepped back from him with a sultry smile, feeling that at last she had him where she wanted him. Totally under her power. 'You're right. It was a great way to start the day.'

Finn dragged himself off the desk, but it looked as though his legs weren't quite up to the task of standing upright. He sent a hand through his hair, leaving deep grooves, his expression one of slight bewilderment. He gave a slow blink as if recalibrating himself, a mercurial smile lifting the edges of his mouth.

'I think I'm going to enjoy working with you way more than I anticipated.' He reached out his hand and picked up one of hers, bringing it up to his mouth, his eyes still locked on hers. He pressed a light kiss to each of her bent knuckles, the delicate caress sending a shower of shivers cascading down her spine.

The reality of what had just happened between them suddenly hit Zoey with the force of a slap. She pulled her hand out of his before she was tempted to do another round of off-the-charts office sex with him. How could she have let her wild side out to such a degree? The wild side she hadn't even known she possessed. It was like looking at a totally different person—a *femme fatale* who was driven by earthly drives and pleasures.

How long could this go on? She was supposed to be working on a project with him—an important project—not making out with him every chance she got. She didn't want to join the long list of Finn's temporary lovers. The flings who came and went in his life with such startling frequency. She hadn't had a fling in her life—she had only ever been in a couple of committed relationships before her ex. She wasn't even sure she liked the idea of casual sex. Where was the humanity in using someone's body to satiate her own desires? Where was the dignity of behaving like an animal without a theory of mind, only driven by raw, primal urges?

'Speaking of work…' Zoey straightened her clothes in a back-to-business manner before bringing her gaze back to his. 'I—I want to make something perfectly clear. I'm not having a fling with you. What happened here—' she waved her hand in the vague direction of his desk '—can't happen again. It's…it's totally unprofessional. It has to stop. Now.'

'Fine. Your call. But let me know as soon as you change your mind.'

Something about his smiling eyes told her he was in no doubt of the struggle she was undergoing. The struggle to keep her hands off him, to be the disciplined professional she had trained herself for so long and hard to be. He had undone it with a single kiss, dismantled her armour like a hurricane through a house of cards.

'I won't be changing my mind,' Zoey said, pointedly ignoring his desk, for it seemed to mock her prim-sounding tone. So too did the secret, silent tremors of her body, the intimate muscles still flicking, kicking, tingling with tiny aftershocks. 'I don't want the distraction, for one thing, nor do I want everyone gossiping about me as your latest squeeze. It would be nothing short of humiliating. I'm here to work and that is what I intend to do.'

'We could always keep it a secret,' Finn said, his gaze unwavering on hers as if reading every betraying nuance on her face.

Zoey folded her arms across her body, desperate to restore some much-needed dignity. She had lost so much ground by falling yet again under his potent sensual spell. As tempting as it was to consider a secret liaison with him, what would happen once it was over? For it would all too soon be over—there was nothing more certain than that. Besides, neither of them wanted anything long-term. That part of her life was over. She had drawn a thick black line through it.

Now wasn't the time to erase it. Now was the time to concentrate on her career, to fulfil her ambitions without the distraction of a relationship.

And a relationship of any duration with Finn would be one hell of a distraction. 'Secrets have a habit of becoming exposed,' she said.

'Not if we're careful.'

But that was the problem right there—she lost her ability to be careful when she was around Finn O'Connell. He triggered something reckless and dangerous in her and she *had* to control it. 'Thanks, but no.'

Finn gave an indifferent shrug and moved back to his desk. He straightened the objects he had pushed aside earlier with maddening casual ease, as if he made hot, passionate love to women on his desk every day. But then, he probably did, and Zoey had now joined their number. *Urgh.* Why had she allowed herself to be swept away on a tide of passion with a man she hated?

But you don't hate him.

The thought dropped into her head and stunned her for a moment. What did she feel for him apart from unbridled lust? Her hatred had cooled a little, more than a little, and in its place was a growing respect for all he had achieved given his difficult childhood. She even had to admit she actually liked some aspects of his personality. His drive and ambition were similar to her own. He worked hard, played hard and could be hard-nosed about business decisions, but didn't she secretly admire that single-mindedness?

And she couldn't forget about his battle-scarred cat. Finn had a caring side, a side he obviously didn't show to people too easily, but Zoey had seen it and liked what she saw.

But Finn had been late this morning and it niggled at the back of her mind that he could well have come straight from another woman's bed. Could she bear the thought of him delivering passionate, planet-dislodging sex so soon after being with another woman?

It reminded her too much of the humiliation of what her ex had done to her. Rupert had made love to her the very same morning before she'd come home and found him in bed with another woman later in the day. The discovery of them in her own bed had made her sick to her stomach. She couldn't rid her brain of the image of their naked bodies wrapped in each other's arms.

Finn pulled his chair out and indicated for her to sit on the chair opposite his desk, his expression now back in business mode. 'Let's nut out a few preliminary ideas for the Frascatelli project.'

Zoey sat on the chair and smoothed her skirt over her knees. 'Can I ask you something first?'

'Sure. Fire away.'

She ran the tip of her tongue across her lips, her gaze drifting to his mouth almost of its own volition. 'Erm…' She gave herself a mental shake and asked, 'Why were you late this morning?'

One corner of his mouth lifted in a half-smile. 'You can blame Tolstoy. I let him outside for a bit of sunshine in the garden, but he climbed up one of the trees and refused to come down.'

Relief swept through Zoey in a whooshing wave that made her slightly dizzy. He hadn't been with another woman. Yay. But then she thought about poor Tolstoy who didn't look strong enough to hold his own outdoors. 'Oh, did you get him back in?' She had a sudden vision of the poor cat getting run over or beaten up by another cat.

'Yeah, eventually.' His smile turned rueful. 'Next time, I'm getting a dog, they're way more obedient.'

'Why did you call him Tolstoy?'

'Because our relationship is one that oscillates between war and peace. We're currently in a war phase but there are peace negotiations in process.' He gave a grin and added, 'I'm hoping for a truce by this evening.'

Zoey laughed. 'Then I hope you're successful.' She was the first to admit he had a great sense of humour. 'I really liked him. He's quite adorable, notwithstanding his war wounds.'

'He was quite taken by you.' Finn's gaze held hers in a spine-tingling lock. 'His loving behaviour was completely out of character. I've had to stop entertaining at home because I'm worried he'll scratch someone. He only just tolerates my housekeeper because she feeds him fillet steak.'

'That must seriously cramp your style. I mean, not being able to have…erm…guests over.' She glanced at his mouth and wondered who would be the next woman to kiss those sculptured lips. Who would be the next woman to scream with pleasure in his arms?

His gaze dipped to her mouth and one side of his mouth came up in a half-smile. 'I manage.'

There was a moment or two of silence.

Zoey tore her gaze away from his mouth and shifted her weight in the chair. 'So, what's your vision for the project?' There—who said she couldn't be single-minded?

He leaned forward to pick up a gold pen from his desk and then leaned back in his chair, flicking the button on the top of the pen on and off. His gaze held hers in an unmistakably intimate tether that made her blood tick and roar in her veins. 'What are the four principles of advertising a product?'

Zoey disguised a swallow. 'Erm…attraction, interest, desire, action.' Exactly what Finn had done to her. Attracted her, piqued her interest, made her desire him and spurned her into action. Sensual, racy action she still couldn't quite believe she had taken. And—God forgive her for being so weak—action she wanted to take again.

A knowing smile ghosted his mouth, his dark eyes containing a smouldering glint that made her heart skip a beat and something topple over in her stomach. 'Foolproof, right?'

She licked her lips again before she could control the impulse. 'Yes.'

He tossed the pen he was clicking back down on the desk. 'We need to work on those principles but ramp up the heat. Most well-travelled people are familiar with the Frascatelli hotel chain in Europe, but we need to show the brand as never before. Leo, as you know, wants to build his brand here in the UK. We need to aim not just for the wow factor, but to convince people a Frascatelli hotel is the only place to stay. Agreed?'

Zoey nodded. 'Agreed.'

They discussed a few more ideas back and forth and Zoey was pleasantly surprised at how well he listened and took on board her opinions. He didn't interrupt or discount what she had to say but encouraged her to expand her ideas, to take them a little further out of her comfort zone. It was nothing like the brainstorming sessions she conducted with her father. Her father had dismissed her opinions, ridiculed her and belittled her when her ideas hadn't aligned with his. But with Finn it was an exhilarating process and she was disappointed when he brought the meeting to a close. The time had grown powerful wings and flown by.

Finn pushed back his chair to stand. 'Let's go away and each do our thing and we'll toss our ideas together some more over dinner tonight. Okay?'

'Okay.' Zoey rose from her chair and hunted around for her bag. She picked it up off the floor and hung the strap over her left shoulder, adding, 'Did you have somewhere in mind? I'll meet you there.'

'Let's do it at my place. It'll be more private. And Tolstoy will enjoy seeing you again.'

Do it? More private? The *double entendre* made Zoey arch her brows. 'We'll be working, not…not doing anything else.'

'But of course,' he said with an enigmatic smile. 'Your call, right?'

Zoey lifted her chin, determined to resist him no matter how irresistible he was. And on a scale of irresistible he was way up at the top.

And she had better not forget it.

CHAPTER SEVEN

For the rest of the day, Finn found his thoughts drifting to the explosive little interlude with Zoey in his office. He couldn't look at his desk without picturing her there, nor could he get his mind away from the image of her going down on him. His whole body shuddered in remembrance, the pleasure so intense it had shaken him to the foundation of his being. Their mutual lust was heady and addictive, and yet Zoey seemed to want him with one hand but push him away with the other.

It was her decision. He wasn't the sort of man to force himself on a woman if she was feeling a little conflicted. But he suspected she was holding him off because she was frightened of the passion he stirred in her. When it came to that, he was a little frightened himself of the things she triggered in him.

Mixing business and pleasure was something he had always shied away from in the past but in

Zoey's case he was prepared to make an exception. He wanted her and he knew damn well she wanted him. He was sure it was only a matter of time before she would be back in his arms. For how long, he couldn't say. His flings were short, brutally short, but he suspected a brief liaison with Zoey was not going to douse the flames of lust she evoked in him any time soon.

Their two explosive encounters had made him even more in lust with her. He wanted her with a ferocity that was all-consuming. She filled his thoughts like an obsession. Her wild sensuality sent a shockwave through his senses, making him thrum with the aftershocks for hours.

Somehow Zoey had done what no other woman had done before—she had taken control of their relationship, dictating when and even if, it would progress.

And the most disturbing thing of all was that he *wanted* it to progress. Wanted it badly. Not for ever, because he wasn't a for ever guy, but he wanted her for now. A fling was all he would offer, but so far, she was holding him at bay on that count. Was that why he was so captivated by her? The thrill of the chase had never been more exciting. The sex was beyond description. The drumming need to have her again was relentless, stirring his senses into a frenzy as soon as he saw her.

Yes, a short fling would be just the thing to

get her out of his system. He couldn't allow a woman—even one as beautiful and delightfully entertaining as Zoey Brackenfield—to get under his skin for too long. Commitment of that sort was anathema to him, but then, apparently it was for her too.

Had someone broken her heart? Her father hadn't mentioned anything to him about a boyfriend, but then Harry didn't often talk much about Zoey other than to criticise her. Finn got the feeling Harry was one of those parents who had no idea how to love and value their offspring. And, unfortunately, Finn knew better than most how that felt.

Finn walked out of his office for the day, and June looked up from her desk with a twinkling smile. 'Zoey Brackenfield is rather stunning, isn't she? Those unusual violet eyes, that beautiful mouth, that gorgeous complexion. How on earth do you keep your hands off her?'

He kept his expression bland, but his lower body leapt at the mention of Zoey's physical attributes. Her beautiful mouth had been around him that morning and had just about blown the top of his head off with its wild magic. She had made him punch-drunk with pleasure. Shaken him, rattled him, scrambled him. And he couldn't wait for her to do it again.

'She's not the fling type.'

'And you're not the marrying type.' June gave a little shrug and added with a sigh, 'Pity.'

Finn affected a laugh. 'Well, nor is she, as it turns out.'

June's eyes danced as if they were auditioning for a reality TV dance show. 'Oh, even better.'

'Why's that?'

'Because she's nothing like all the other women who look up to you like you're some sort of rock god. She's seeing the real you, not the idealised you. She's seeing you as an equal, and that makes for a much better relationship in the long term.'

'Ahem.' Finn pointedly cleared his throat. 'Who said anything about a long-term relationship?'

June's smile was undented by his savage frown or curt tone. 'Just putting it out there.'

'I pay you to work for me, not to comment on my private life.'

'And just how satisfying has your private life been over the last few months?'

'Very satisfying.' But not before he had met Zoey. Finn suddenly realised he hadn't felt properly alive before he met her. His day to day, week to week, month to month routine had gradually become so humdrum. He hadn't noticed until Zoey had brought colour, energy and zing to his life. Their occasional meetings at various advertising gigs had been the bright spots in his otherwise routine existence. And just lately she had awakened a dormant part of him, stirring it into living, breathing vitality.

'Zoey Brackenfield is a breath of fresh air,' June said, as if reading his thoughts. 'I think she'll be an asset to the company.' Her smile became enigmatic. 'Who knows how she will shake this place up, hey?'

Who indeed? But, if what had happened between him and Zoey so far was any indication, all he could say was, *Bring it on.*

Zoey dressed with care for her dinner at Finn's house. She spent ages on her hair and make-up, making sure she looked her best. She wasn't game enough to question why she was going to so much trouble—after all, she was supposed to be keeping things strictly business between them.

But every time she thought of him—which was way too often for her liking—her mind filled with images of them in his office making mad, passionate love. Her body remembered every glide of his hands, every stroke and flicker of his tongue against her most tender and sensitive flesh. She shivered as she recalled the taste of him, the feel of him, the velvet and steel power of him and how he was completely undone by her caresses. Which was only fair, seeing how undone she had been by his.

She was starting to realise she had seriously

misjudged Finn in every way possible. She had accused him of betraying her over the takeover of her father's company, but a subsequent conversation with her father had confirmed what Finn had said—her father had approached Finn, not the other way round. There was so much more to Finn than she had first thought. He had a depth of character that intrigued her and pleased her. He wasn't the shallow, self-serving man she had assumed him to be.

Zoey picked up her evening bag and gave herself one more glance in the full-length mirror. The black dress wasn't new, but it outlined her curves without revealing too much cleavage. She had washed and blow-dried her hair, leaving it loose and wavy around her shoulders. Her make-up was understated apart from smoky eyeliner and a vivid slash of red lipstick.

'You'll do,' she said to her reflection. 'But don't get any funny ideas about tonight. It's a working dinner, nothing else.'

Finn answered the door to her dressed in camel-coloured trousers and a casual white shirt that highlighted the width of his shoulders. His hair was still damp from a recent shower and his jaw freshly shaven. 'Wow. You look good enough to eat,' he said with a glinting smile.

Zoey suppressed a shiver and stepped across

the threshold, shooting him a narrow glance on the way past. 'Don't even think about it, O'Connell. I'm here to work, not play.'

'Spoilsport.' Finn grinned and then closed the door behind her. 'Come this way—I'm just putting the finishing touches to our meal.'

Zoey followed him to the well-appointed kitchen at the rear of the house, its bank of windows overlooking the garden. She looked at the various items he was preparing on the large island countertop—fillet steaks marinated in red wine and herbs, a melange of green vegetables, potatoes Dauphinoise, as well as a delectable cheese board with seasonal fruit. 'Impressive. I didn't know you were so domesticated. I thought you'd get your housekeeper to do that for you.'

'She only comes in to clean once a week and to look after Tolstoy when I travel.'

Zoey glanced around the room. 'Where is he?'

'Sulking upstairs.' Finn reached for a couple of wine glasses in a cupboard and then placed them on the countertop. 'I wouldn't let him go outside after this morning's *contretemps*.' He held up a bottle of red wine. 'I have white if you'd prefer.'

'Red is fine, thank you.' Zoey perched on one of the stools next to the island bench.

He poured two glasses of the red wine and handed her one, holding his up to hers in a toast. 'So, to working, not playing, together.' There was a hint of amusement lurking in the background of his dark brown gaze.

Zoey clinked her glass against his, something in her stomach pitching. But would *she* be able to stick to the rules? Her lower body quivered with the memory of his lovemaking, little pulses and flickers that reminded her of the exquisite magic of his touch. And how much she wanted to feel it again. 'Cheers,' she said, her gaze slipping away from the smouldering heat of his.

Finn took a sip of his wine and then placed the glass down as he continued preparing their meal. 'I'm interviewing the key staff at Brackenfield over the next month. I'll offer redundancy packages where it's appropriate, but I plan to do a complete restructure to streamline things to increase efficiency. As a result, some jobs will no longer exist.'

Zoey frowned. 'But some people have been with us for decades. You can't just get rid of them.'

'It's nothing personal, it's a business decision. Increasing profit and mitigating losses have to take priority over everything else.'

'Oh, and I suppose you'll suddenly decide my job no longer exists,' Zoey said, shooting him a glare.

'On the contrary, I'm going to keep you.' He wiped his hands on a tea towel and added, 'June would never speak to me again if I let you go.'

'Could you at least discuss with me first some of the decisions you're making over staff? I know everyone and their skill set and their personal circumstances.'

'Your opinion is likely to be too subjective,' Finn said. 'I don't care what a person's circumstances are—what I care about is whether they are capable of doing their job. I'm running a business, Zoey, not a charity.'

Zoey put her glass of wine down on the counter with a loud thwack. 'Running a business doesn't have to be all about profit. You wouldn't have a business if it weren't for the people you employ. How can you expect to get the best from them if you only see them as cogs in a wheel instead of as human beings? People who have families to feed, difficulties to overcome, mortgages and rent to pay—'

'And I suppose the way you and your father have run Brackenfield Advertising with all that touchy-feely stuff has worked well for you?' His gaze was direct, hard and penetrating.

Zoey couldn't hold his gaze and jumped down from the stool to walk over to the windows and look at the garden lit up with various lights. Anger rumbled through her at his cold-hearted approach to business but, as he said, had her father's way been any better?

Her father had pretended to care about his employees but had exploited them on many occasions, just as he'd exploited her, relying on her to do his work for him, to cover for him, to make excuses for him. She had bent herself out of shape to please him, to keep the company going, yet it had all been for nothing. Just as she had done for Rupert—over-adapting to make things work, when all the time behind her back he was cheating on her.

'I didn't have much to do with running the company,' she said, still with her back to Finn. 'My father refused to make me a director, believing it was a man's job, not a woman's, and especially not a young woman's. He wanted a son, not a daughter, and has spent the last twenty-eight years reminding me of his bitter disappointment.'

She swung round to look at him and added, 'So, maybe if I'd been able to do things my way, we wouldn't have had to sell to you at all.'

Finn let out a long sigh and came over to where she was standing. 'Your father's a fool for not giving you more responsibility. But, even if you had been able to do things your way, it doesn't change the fact that businesses have to produce profit otherwise they go under. And then everyone loses—owners, staff, shareholders, even the community at large.'

Zoey flicked him an irritated glance from beneath partially lowered lashes. Everything he said was true to a point, but how could she stand by and watch long-term staff be dismissed as if they didn't matter? They mattered to her. 'I just think there are ways to conduct a restructure without destroying people's lives, that's all.'

Finn reached for one of her hands and held it between both of his. 'Look at me, Zoey.' His voice was low and had a softer quality in it than she had heard before. She lifted her gaze to his and her pulse rate picked up as his thumb began a gentle stroking over the back of her hand. His touch was electrifying, sending tiny shivers down her spine. 'It's not my goal to destroy people's lives,' he went on. 'My goal is to—'

Zoey pulled roughly out of his hold. 'Make money. Yeah, yeah, yeah. I heard you the first time.' She rubbed at her hand in a pointed manner, shooting him another glare. 'I've put everything into my father's business. I've worked so damn hard, and you come sweeping in and want to change it all. There'll be nothing left to show for all the sacrifices I've made. Brackenfield Advertising will be swallowed up by your company. It will be as if it never existed.'

'I'm not sure what your understanding of a takeover is, but it's not like a merger,' Finn said, frowning. 'And, let me remind you, this was a friendly takeover, not a hostile one. Your father couldn't wait to sign on the line once I named a sum.'

'But you didn't even give me a hint of what was

going on.' Zoey banged her fist against her chest for emphasis. 'Why was I kept out of the loop? You had the chance to tell me and yet you didn't.'

He muttered a curse not quite under his breath. 'It seems to me this anger of yours is misdirected. You need to address this with your father, not me. I told him he should involve you, but he wouldn't hear of it.'

Zoey swung away from him, wishing now she hadn't agreed to have dinner with him. 'You don't understand how hard this is for me. I've waited all my life for a chance to prove myself to my father and you've come marching in and taken it all away.'

'Why is it so important for you to prove yourself to him?'

Zoey momentarily closed her eyes in a tight blink, her arms wrapped around the middle of her body. 'Because he's all the family I've got.'

Finn came up behind her and, placing his hands on the tops of her shoulders, gently turned her to face him. His gaze had softened, his expression etched in concern. 'What about your mother?'

Zoey let out a ragged sigh. 'She died when I was four. Horse accident. I was at nursery school when it happened. She never regained consciousness. My father didn't let me see her in hospital or allow me to go to her funeral. He thought it would upset me too much. But it upset me more by not being able to say goodbye to her.'

Finn wrapped his arms around her and brought her close against his body. He rested his chin on the top of her head, one of his hands gently stroking the back of her head in a comforting manner. 'I'm sorry. That must have been pretty tough on you.'

Zoey leant her cheek against his broad chest, the citrus notes of his aftershave tantalising her nostrils, the steely strength of his arms around her soothing and protective.

'I was lucky that I had nice stepmothers and nannies over the years. Dad remarried several times, I guess in the attempt to have the son he always wanted, not that it ever happened. Only one of his new wives got pregnant but she had a miscarriage and didn't try again, but left him soon after.' She sighed and added, 'I've never been enough for my dad. He wanted a son to pass the business on to and instead got me. And now it's too late.'

'He should be more than happy with you,' Finn said, kissing the top of her head. 'And what's this talk of it being too late?' He eased her away from him to look down at her with a reproving frown. 'You don't need your father to be successful. You can do it on your own. You're talented, Zoey, really talented. You bring a lot of innovation to your projects. They're fresh and original, and I'm sure it won't be long before you get the credit you deserve.'

Zoey basked in the glow of his confidence in her. It was so rare for her to hear praise other than from her close friends and hearing it from Finn, whom she respected and admired professionally, was like breathing in clean air after a lifetime of pollution. 'It's nice of you to say so.'

His brows lifted in a mock-surprised manner. 'Nice? Me?'

Zoey gave a rueful smile. 'You're nice enough to allow me to bore you with all my baggage.'

He lifted her chin with the end of his finger, his eyes dark and unwavering on hers. 'I'm beginning to think it's impossible for you to ever bore me.' His gaze dipped to her mouth and the atmosphere tightened as if all the oxygen particles in the room had disappeared.

Zoey moistened her lips, her eyes going to the sculpted perfection of his mouth. Her lips began to tingle in anticipation, and a soft but insistent beat of desire fluttered like wings deep in her core. 'Oh, I don't think I'm all that exciting…' She touched his lean jaw with her fingers, trailing them down to his lips. 'You, on the other hand…' Her voice dropped down to a whisper.

He captured her hand and held it up to his face, pressing a kiss to the middle of her palm, his eyes still holding hers. 'Is this working or playing?' His tone was gently teasing, his smile doing serious damage to her resolve to resist him.

But how could she resist him? He was a drug she hadn't known she had a penchant for until she kissed him the first time. Now her ardent need of him was a driving force that refused to go away. Every time she was around him, the craving intensified.

Zoey pressed herself a little closer, her lower body coming into intimate contact with his growing erection. 'I don't know why this keeps happening between us. I keep telling myself I won't give in to temptation and then I go ahead and do it.'

'I can tell you why.' He smoothed his hand down from below her shoulder blades to the small of her back, pressing her harder into his arousal. 'Because we both want each other.'

Zoey let out a shuddery breath, the heat of his body calling out to hers with a fierce, primal energy. 'I don't want a relationship with anyone right now. Maybe not ever.'

He tipped up her chin, locking his gaze back on hers. 'Why?'

She bit down into her lower lip, those horrid images inside her head of her ex with his new lover torturing her all over again. 'My ex cheated on me. It had been happening for months. I came home and found him in our bed with her.' She closed her eyes in a tight blink and then opened them again to add, 'He'd even made love to me that same morning. Told me he loved me and all.'

Finn held her apart from him, his frowning gaze holding hers. 'That is truly despicable. I'm not surprised you're so against getting involved with anyone again.'

Zoey looked at his chin rather than meet his gaze. 'I thought things were fine between us. I mean, we'd been together for years. But, looking back, there were lots of red flags I didn't notice at the time.' Her gaze crept back to his. 'It's only since you and I hooked up that I've realised how boring my sex life with him was. Maybe that's why he strayed. I wasn't exciting enough for him.'

Finn grasped her by the upper arms in a gentle but firm hold. 'Don't go blaming yourself for his shortcomings, Zoey. You're by far the most exciting lover I've ever had. He was the one who chose to cheat rather than discuss any concerns he might have had. You're better off without him.'

'Yes, well, I know that, but I just don't feel ready to date seriously again.'

'The life of having hook-ups isn't always what it's cracked up to be,' Finn said with a rueful grimace. 'It too can get a little boring.'

Zoey arched her eyebrows. 'Don't tell me the hardened playboy is looking for more permanent pastures on which to graze?'

He gave a crooked smile. 'Not a chance.' His hands slipped back down to hold her by the hips. 'But I'm not averse to having the odd extended fling from time to time.'

Zoey began to toy with one of the buttons on his shirt. 'How long do your, erm, extended flings normally last?' She flicked him a glance and added, 'I'm asking for a friend.'

Finn laughed and brought her closer to his body. 'Well, let's see now… I had one that lasted for a month once, but it was a long time ago.'

'Were you in love with her?' The question was out before Zoey could monitor her tongue. Was he capable of loving someone to that degree? Or was love something he avoided out of the fear of being hurt as his parents had hurt him?

'No. I've never experienced that feeling.'

'Would you recognise it if you did?'

'Would you?' His gaze was suddenly too direct, too penetrating, for her to hold.

Zoey looked back at the button she was playing with on his shirt. 'I'm not sure… I really thought I was in love with Rupert, but I can see now that I just cared about him as a person.'

She glanced up at him again. 'My two ex-flatmates have both recently fallen madly in love with their partners. I don't think I felt anything like what they feel for their new fiancés. And I am doubly sure Rupert never, ever looked at me the way my friends' fiancés look at them. As if the world would be an empty place without them in it.'

Finn slid one of his hands up to the nape of her neck, his fingers warm and gentle against her skin. 'Love can be a beautiful thing when it happens.'

She angled her head at him. 'So, you actually believe it can happen?'

His fingers splayed through her hair, sending a shiver down her spine. 'I too have a couple of friends who've been lucky enough to find love with each other.' His lips made a twisted movement. 'But of course, whether it lasts is another question. So many marriages end in divorce.'

'But your parents didn't divorce?'

He made a soft, snorting noise. 'They never tied the knot in the first place. They broke up a couple of times but drifted back together as drinking and drug buddies. Or so I'm told—I haven't seen them since I was thirteen.'

Zoey frowned and reached up to touch his face with her hand. 'I can only imagine how devastated you must have been by them behaving so irresponsibly. Do you know why they became like that? What were their backgrounds like? People who grow up in difficult circumstances often replicate them in their own lives as adults.'

Finn removed his hand from her hair and placed it on the top of her shoulder. His expression became stony, impenetrable. 'I get a little tired of people who excuse their appalling behaviour on their backgrounds. We all have choices in how we behave.'

'I know, but it can be really hard for some people to push past the stuff that happened to them, especially in early childhood,' Zoey said. 'Children's brains can be affected by witnessing violence or experiencing abuse. It can have a lifelong impact.'

Finn stepped away from her as if the conversation was causing him discomfort. He scraped a hand through his hair, his mouth tightly set. 'Look, I know you mean well, but if you're thinking I'll ever have a nice, cosy little reunion with my parents, then you're completely mistaken. I want nothing to do with either of them or the relatives that brought me up.'

Something in Zoey's stomach dropped. 'Why are you so hard on your relatives? Were they...abusive?' She hated even saying the word, wondering if Finn had suffered at the hands of his carers in the most despicable way.

He gave a short, embittered laugh. 'Depends what you mean by abusive. No one ever laid a hand on me, and I was always fed and clothed, but I was left in no doubt of how much of an inconvenience I was to them. I got passed around three or four families over the years. No one wanted to keep me any length of time. They had their own kids, their own tight little family unit, and I didn't belong.'

'Oh, Finn,' Zoey said. 'What about your grand-parents? Did either set have—?'

'My father was disowned by his parents for his lifestyle choices. My mother's parents had me for the occasional weekend in the early years but found the task of taking care of a young child too taxing, especially a child born out of wedlock. They were highly religious and were not averse to telling me I was the spawn of the devil. Both of them died within a couple of years of each other and I was farmed out to various great-aunts and great-uncles.' He gave a grim smile and added, 'The only contact I have with any of them is when they ask for money.'

Zoey frowned. 'Do you give it to them?'

He came back to place his hands on her shoulders, his eyes meshing with hers. 'I don't want to talk about my family any more. This is what I'd rather do.' And he brought his mouth down to hers.

CHAPTER EIGHT

FINN WONDERED IF he would ever tire of kissing Zoey's soft and responsive lips. He loved the taste of her, the smell of her skin, the touch of her hands, the way her body pressed against his, as if she wanted to melt into him completely.

But it wasn't just the physical closeness with her that stirred him so deeply. It was the strange sense of camaraderie he felt with her. Both of them were only children who hadn't had things easy and both of them were relentlessly driven to achieve, to prove something to themselves, to leave an indelible mark on the world. He had never felt such affinity with anyone before and it made him wonder if he was getting too close to her. He was allowing her too much access to his locked-down emotional landscape. The barren wasteland of his childhood was normally something even he didn't revisit. But he had allowed Zoey in and it had changed something in their relationship.

Relationship? Was that what this was between them? He didn't do relationships as such. Not the ones that stretched into the future without an end point. He only conducted temporary relationships that didn't go deep enough to engage his emotions. The sort of emotions that made him vulnerable in the way he had been as a child—wanting love, needing it, craving it and yet repeatedly being denied it.

He had taught himself to ignore the human need to be loved. To ignore the need to be connected in such a deep and lasting way to another person. The sort of love that made your bones ache to be with the other person. The sort of love that filled your chest and made it hard to take a breath without feeling its tug. The sort of love that could be snatched away when you needed it the most, leaving you empty, abandoned, vulnerable. And that most awful word of all—lonely.

Finn was not the 'falling in love with your soul mate' type. He had never pictured himself growing old with someone, having a family and doing all the things that long-term couples do. His career was his focus, continuing to build his empire that provided more money than he could spend and gave him more accolades than he could ever have dreamed of receiving.

And yet, with Zoey's mouth beneath his, and her arms around his body, her soft whimpers of pleasure made him wonder if going back to his casual approach to sex was going to be as exciting as it once had been. He was finding it increasingly hard to imagine making love with someone else. Found it hard to imagine how he would desire anyone else with anywhere near the same fervour he had for her. It was as relentless as his drive to succeed, maybe even more so. And that was deeply disturbing.

Zoey lifted her mouth off his to gaze into his eyes. Her cheeks were flushed, her lips swollen from the pressure of his, and he could not think of a moment when she had looked more beautiful. 'I hope the dinner you've been preparing isn't burning to a crisp.'

Finn had completely forgotten about the meal—the only hunger he felt was for her. A rabid hunger then clawed at his very being. He framed her face with his hands and kissed the tip of her nose. 'You have the amazing ability to distract me.'

Her lips curved in a smile. 'Likewise.' But then a tiny frown flickered across her forehead and she added with a slight drop of her gaze, 'I'm not sure what's happening between us…'

Finn knew what *he* wanted to happen—more of what was already happening. The electric energy of being intimate with her, the blood-pumping passion of holding her, the thrill of his senses each time he looked at her. He wanted her like he had wanted no one before. But would the occasional hook-up with her truly satisfy him? For the first time in his life, he wanted to indulge in a longer relationship. Not long-term, but longer than he normally would.

But would Zoey agree to it?

'What do you want to happen between us?' Finn could barely believe he was asking such a loaded question. A dangerous question. He was giving her control over the very thing he *always* controlled—when a relationship started and when it ended.

She ran the tip of her tongue across her lips, her gaze creeping back up to meet his. 'Nothing permanent.'

Nothing permanent. Hearing his own words coming out of her mouth should have delighted him, and would have delighted him if anyone other than her had said it. He was the one who normally set the rules of a relationship, and yet this time Zoey wanted that privilege. And, because he wanted her so badly, he would give it to her without question. 'Okay. So, a fling for as long as we both want it. Does that sound workable?'

Her teeth sank into the fleshy part of her lower lip for a moment. Then her eyes meshed with his with a spark of intractability. 'As long as we both agree to be exclusive. That for me is not negotiable.'

Finn couldn't agree more. He hadn't been too

keen on an open relationship—call him old-fashioned, but he wasn't into sharing, especially when it was Zoey, the woman of his sensual dreams and fantasies. The thought of her with anyone else churned his gut, which was surprising to him, because he had never considered himself the jealous type. He had no time for possessive men who thought they owned a woman, but something about Zoey made him want her all to himself.

'It's a deal-breaker for me too. I might be fairly casual with how I conduct my sex life, but I have never played around on a current partner.'

A smile flickered at the edges of her mouth and her arms wound back around his waist. 'I've never had a fling before. I've always been in long-term relationships. Don't you find it ironic that you're the opposite?'

Finn gave a wry grin. 'Believe me, the irony hasn't escaped me.' He brought her closer, hip to hip, pelvis to pelvis, need to need. 'I have an idea. Can you clear your diary for next week?'

'I might be able to, why?'

'I want to be alone with you, somewhere without distractions,' Finn said. 'How does Monte Carlo sound?'

Her eyes lowered from his, her teeth beginning to chew at her lower lip. 'It sounds lovely but…'

He tipped up her chin, so her gaze met his. 'But?'

A flicker of something passed through her gaze. 'It's tempting.'

'That's the whole point.'

She gave a half-smile. 'It sounds wonderful. I haven't been there before, but I've always wanted to go.' But then her smile faded and a frown took up residence on her forehead. 'But what about Tolstoy?'

'I'll get my housekeeper to look after him.' He gave a grimace and added, 'It'll put the peace negotiations back a bit, but hopefully he'll forgive me.'

Zoey made a sad face. 'Poor boy. Cats don't like change and regularly punish their owners when there's a change of routine.'

'Yes, so I'm finding out. You're the only person I've been able to have here since I got him. It will seriously curtail my social life if he doesn't improve his attitude.'

Zoey studied him for a moment. 'If he's turning out to be so much trouble, why haven't you given him to someone else?'

'After all the money I spent on him? No way. He can damn well adjust. I've had to.'

Her lips began to twitch with another smile. 'You love him.'

Finn hadn't really thought about it before, but it suddenly occurred to him that he had developed an attachment to that wretched cat. The thing wasn't even cute and cuddly. It looked more like something out of a horror movie. But he had grown to look forward to seeing Tolstoy at the start and end of each day, even if he wasn't the most congenial housemate. 'Yeah, well, maybe I've developed a mild affection for him.'

Zoey's smile became playful. 'So, the ruthless businessman has a heart after all. Who knew?'

Finn gave her a look. 'Not so big a heart that I would consent to taking him with me to Monte Carlo. I do have my limits. Besides, I want you to myself. My villa is private and secluded, and I often go there when I need to work on a deadline. And, given that Leo Frascatelli has plans for a hotel revamp in Nice, which is only a few minutes' drive away, we can do some on-site research.'

A tiny frown tugged at her forehead. 'But won't having me there be a distraction?'

Finn pressed a kiss to her mouth. 'A shocking one, but I think I can handle it.'

A sparkling light came into her eyes and her arms moved from around his waist to link around his neck. 'You think you can handle me?' Her tone was teasing, her touch electric, and he wished he could clear his diary for a month instead of a week and spend it alone with her. 'You have no idea what you're letting yourself in for, O'Connell.' She pressed her lips against his for a brief moment, making him desperate for more. 'Don't say you weren't warned.'

'Warning heeded,' Finn said and brought his mouth back down on hers.

The following day, Zoey met up with Ivy and Millie for a quick catch-up over a drink after work. She always looked forward to catching up with her friends but, since they had both become so happily engaged, she felt a little on the outer. The irony was, she had once been the marrying type. It was why she had been with Rupert for so long—seven years. Every year that had passed without him presenting her with an engagement ring she had made excuses for him. He was under the pump at work…he wasn't ready for marriage yet…he wanted to pay off some debts first. She had spent years of her life waiting, only to have her loyalty and commitment thrown back in her face.

And now, she was the one who didn't want to settle down.

'Millie told me about your little hook-up in New York with Finn O'Connell,' Ivy said with a smile. 'You do realise I fell in love with Louis after a one-night stand?'

Zoey gave her a droll look. 'I'm not going to fall in love with Finn O'Connell, okay?' She was in lust with him and it was wonderful. She had never felt like this before, so alive and in touch with her body. When he had first suggested the trip, she had been assailed with doubts. Would she be setting herself up for hurt by spending such concentrated time with him? But she reassured herself it was just a fling. She was the one in control and she would stay in control. Five days with him in Monte Carlo would be divine. It was just what she needed right now, a chance to put some of her past disappointments aside and enjoy herself by living in the moment.

Millie leaned forward to pick up one of the nibbles from the plate in front of them. 'How will you stop yourself? I said the same thing about Hunter. When love strikes, it strikes, and you can't do anything to stop it.'

Zoey topped up her wine from the bottle on the table. 'I don't think I've ever been in love, or at least not like you two are. What I felt for Rupert was… I don't know… I told him I loved him plenty of times, and he did me, but…'

'But?' Millie and Ivy spoke together.

Ivy blew out a little breath and twirled the wine around in her glass. 'I think I might have been in love with the idea of being in love. Of being important to someone, you know? Really important to them, not just someone they lived with who did the bulk of the cooking and cleaning and was available for sex whenever they wanted it.' She gave the girls a wincing look and asked, 'Too much information?'

'You've never really talked about your relationship with Rupert so honestly before,' Ivy said.

'Maybe acknowledging the problems you had with him will help you to not to repeat the mistakes in a future relationship.'

'That's exactly what I'm doing,' Zoey said. 'I'm doing what I want for a change. That's why a fling with Finn O'Connell is perfect for me right now. We want the same things—a no-strings, no-rings, no-promises-of-for-ever fling.'

'So, will you bring him to my wedding as your plus-one?' Ivy asked, looking hopeful.

Zoey gave a short laugh. 'I'm not sure a romantic wedding would be Finn O'Connell's thing at all. Besides, I don't want to broadcast it too publicly that I'm having a fling with him.'

Ivy and Millie exchanged speaking looks. Zoey frowned at them both. 'What?'

'Are you sure a fling is all you want from Finn?' Ivy asked, with a look of concern. 'Have you really changed that much to go from having a long-term relationship history to wanting nothing but flings with people who take your fancy?'

'Of course I've changed,' Zoey said. 'No offence to you two, but I can't see myself settling down with someone any more.' The inevitable hurt, the vulnerability, the crushing disappointment when the person you had committed your life to let you down. Why would she sign up for that? It was better this way, she had way more control.

'I think it's sad that you feel that way,' Ivy said.

'I can't wait to spend the rest of my life with Louis. To think I might have missed out on feeling like this about someone and have him feel the same way about me is too awful to contemplate.'

'But what if Finn wants more?' Millie chimed in.

'Not a chance,' Zoey reassured her and reached for a marinated olive from the plate. 'He's a playboy with no desire to settle down.' She popped the olive in her mouth and chewed and swallowed. 'Look, be happy for me, okay? I'm spending the next five days with him in Monte Carlo. It's kind of a working holiday but there'll be plenty of time for…other stuff.'

Millie and Ivy exchanged *can you believe this?* looks and Zoey rolled her eyes. 'What is it with you two? No one is going to fall in love, okay?'

'We just don't want you to get hurt, Zoey,' Millie said. 'You've been through a lot with Rupert and your dad. The last thing you need is to get your heart broken again.'

'Don't worry, it won't get broken.' Zoey wondered now if it was her pride that had been hurt rather than her heart when it came to her ex.

And, as long as she kept her pride intact during her time with Finn, she would be perfectly safe.

Finn and Zoey flew the next day from London to Nice and then drove the twenty-minute drive to his villa in Monte Carlo in a luxury hire car. Zoey stepped out of the car and gazed at the Belle Époque style three-storey villa, with glossy, black wrought-iron balconies on the two upper levels. She had thought his London home was stunning, but this was on a whole new level.

'Oh, wow, it's lovely…' she said, shading her eyes with her hand from the brilliant sunshine to take in the view over the water in the distance.

Finn placed his hand on the small of her back to guide her forward towards the villa. 'I'm glad you like it.'

'How could anyone not?' She stepped inside the villa and turned a full circle in the marble foyer. A large crystal chandelier hung from the tall ceiling. The floor was beautifully polished parquetry, partially covered with a luxurious Persian rug that picked up the black and white and gold theme of the décor. A large gilt-edged mirror on one wall made the foyer seem even more commodious than it was, and that was saying something, because it was huge. There were works of art on the walls that very much looked like originals and there were fresh flowers in a whimsical arrangement on a black-trimmed marble table in front of the grand, sweeping staircase.

Zoey turned back to face him. 'Oh, Finn, this is truly the most amazing place. How long have you had it?'

'A year or two. It was a little run-down when I bought it, but it's come up well.'

'It certainly has.'

'Why don't you have a look around while I bring in the bags?' Finn said. 'The garden and pool are that way.' He pointed to the right of the grand staircase, where she could see a glimpse of lush green foliage through a window.

Zoey walked through the villa until she came to a set of French doors leading out to the garden and pool area. Finn hadn't been wrong in describing the villa as secluded and private—the pool and garden were completely so. A tall hedge framed two sides of the property, and the twenty-metre pool in the centre overlooked the sparkling azure-blue of the Mediterranean Sea in the distance. The garden beds in front of the tall hedges either side of the pool were a less structured affair with scented gardenias and colourful azaleas. There was an al fresco dining and lounge seating area on one side, and a cleverly concealed changing room and shower and toilet nearby.

Zoey bent down to test the water temperature of the pool just as Finn came out to join her. 'Fancy a swim?' he asked.

She straightened and smiled at him. 'Don't tempt me.'

He came over to her and took her by the hands, his warm, strong fingers curling around hers. 'Look who's talking. Do you know the effort it took for me to keep my hands off you during that flight?'

A frisson coursed through her body at the glinting look in his dark gaze. 'It took an effort on my part too.'

He brought her closer to the hardened ridge of his growing erection, his hands settling on her hips. A shockwave of awareness swept through her body, desire leaping in her core with pulsing, flickering heat. 'Take your clothes off.' His commanding tone sent her pulse rate soaring.

'What, here? What if someone's watching?'

He smiled a devilish smile. 'I'll be the only one watching.'

Zoey shivered in anticipation, for she knew without a single doubt he would more than deliver on the sensual promise glinting in his gaze. 'I've never gone skinny dipping before. In fact, there's quite a few things I haven't done before I met you. You seem to bring out a wild side in me I didn't know I possessed.'

'I happen to like your wild side.' He brought his mouth down to the shell of her ear, gently taking her earlobe between his teeth and giving it a soft bite. A shiver raced down her spine with lightning-fast speed and a wave of longing swept through her. He lifted his head to lock his gaze back on hers and added, 'It turns me on.'

Zoey moved her lower body against the proud

ridge of his arousal, her blood thrumming with excitement. 'You turn me on too.' She began to unbutton his shirt, button by button, leaving light little kisses against each section of the muscled chest that she uncovered. 'You taste like salt and sun and something else I've never tasted before.'

He became impatient and tugged his shirt out of his jeans and pulled it over his head, tossing it to one side. 'And do you like it?'

'Love it.' She pressed another kiss to his right pectoral muscle. 'I think I might be addicted to it.' She circled his flat male nipple with the point of her tongue, round and round and round. He made a growling sound deep in his throat and she lifted her head to give him a sultry smile. 'Steady… I'm only just getting started.'

'Yeah, well, so am I.' Finn slid the zipper at the back of her sundress down to just above her bottom. The dress slipped off her shoulders and fell to her feet, leaving her in just balcony bra and lacy knickers. He ran his hands over the curve of her bottom, bringing her back against his hardened flesh, his eyes darkening with unbridled lust.

'I'm not taking the rest off until you take off your jeans and underwear.'

His mouth tilted in a smile and he stepped back to strip them. 'Happy now?'

Zoey drank her fill of his gloriously tanned and toned and aroused body, her insides coiling tightly with lust. 'Getting there…' She stroked her fingers down his turgid length in a lightly teasing manner, and he sucked in a harsh-sounding breath and closed his eyes in a slow blink. She cupped him in her hand and massaged up and down, emboldened by the flickers of pleasure passing across his features.

He made another growling sound and pulled her hand away. He reached around her to unfasten her bra, tossing it in the same direction as the rest of his clothes. He hooked his finger in the side of her knickers, drawing them down until they were around her ankles. She stepped out of them and he ran his hungry gaze over her lingeringly while her body throbbed and ached for his possession. No one had ever made her feel so proud of her body. No one had ever triggered such sensual heat and desire in her flesh. No one had ever made her want them with an ache so powerful. It consumed her totally, it drove out every thought but how to get her needs satisfied. It turned her into a wild and wanton being, driven by primal urges.

Finn cupped her breasts in his hands, moving his thumbs over her already peaking nipples. Her flesh tingled at his touch, tingling sensations coursing through her body in an electric current. She made a soft sound of approval, her breathing increasing as the tingles travelled all the way to her core. He bent his head to caress her breast with his lips and tongue, the exquisite torture making her breathless with excitement. His touch was neither too soft or too hard but perfectly in tune with her body's needs.

It was as if he was reading her flesh, intuitively understanding the subtle differences and needs in each of her erogenous zones. He brought his mouth to her other breast in the same masterful manner and a host of sensations rippled through her. Delicious sensations that made her legs tremble and her heart race.

Finn lifted his mouth from her breast and gazed down at her with smouldering eyes. And, without a word, he scooped her up in his arms and carried her to the sun loungers, laying her down on the largest one, which was the size of a double bed. He came down beside her, one of his hands caressing her abdomen, moving slowly, so torturously slowly, towards the throbbing heat of her mound.

'I love watching how your pupils flare when I touch you like this,' he said in a husky tone. 'You have such expressive eyes. They are such an unusual colour, like winter violets. They're either shooting daggers at me or looking at me like you are now.' He brought his mouth down to the edge of hers and teased her with a barely touching kiss. 'Like you can't wait for me to be inside you.'

'Newsflash,' Zoey said, stroking her hand down the length of his spine, her own body on fire. 'I can't wait. Please, please, please make love to me before I go crazy.'

He tapped a gentle finger on the end of her nose. 'Safety first.' He pushed himself up off the lounger and went to get a condom from his wallet in the back pocket of his jeans. Zoey watched him apply it, her need for him at fever pitch.

He came back and joined her on the lounger, his weight propped on one elbow, his other hand stroking her from the indentation of her waist to the flank of her thigh and back again. 'Now, where was I?'

Zoey pulled his head down so his mouth was just above hers. 'You were here.'

Finn's mouth covered hers at the same time he entered her with a deep, thick thrust that made her shiver from head to foot. The movement of his body in hers was slow at first, then built to a crescendo. Her senses rioted, her feminine flesh gripping him tightly, the exquisite tension in her swollen tissues building and building. She rocked with him, her legs tangled with his, her hands stroking the hard contours of his back and shoulders. And then, as she got closer and closer to the point of no return, she grasped him by the buttocks and arched her spine to receive each driving thrust of his body.

Finn slipped his hand between their bodies, caressing her intimately to push her over the edge of the cliff to paradise. She fell apart with a sobbing, panting cry that rent the air, her body quaking as the pulsating sensations went through her. Her orgasm was powerful, overwhelming, earth-shattering and mind-altering, and it went on and on, faded a little and then resumed with even more force. Finn rode out the second wave of her pleasure with his own release, his deep, urgent thrusts triggering yet another explosive orgasm that left her breathless, panting and wondering how on earth her body was capable of such intense pleasure.

Zoey flung her head back against the sun lounger, her chest still rising and falling, the warmth of the sun on her face and the heat of Finn's body lying over her a blessed weight, anchoring her to the earth. It didn't seem possible to experience such profound pleasure without a price to pay and she suddenly realised what it might be. Her earlier hatred of Finn had faded to a less potent dislike, then somehow it had morphed into a deep respect of him. A growing admiration for the things he had overcome to become the man he was today.

And there was another step she was desperately trying to avoid taking—the step towards love. Not just the friendship or casual love, but the sort of love that sent down deep roots into your very being until you couldn't move or breathe without feeling it. The sort of love that made it impossible to imagine life without that person by your side. The sort of love her friends were experiencing with their partners.

A once in a lifetime love.

The sort of love Zoey had never experienced before… How had she settled for all those years with her ex when she hadn't felt anything like what she was beginning to feel for Finn? The feelings inside her were like the first stumbling steps of a toddler learning to walk. Tentative, uncertain, unstable. But how could she be sure it was actually the real deal—love? What if she was confusing great sex with long-lasting love? It was an easy mistake, and many women made it, becoming swept up in the heady rush of a new relationship when the sex was exciting and fresh and deeply satisfying.

Finn propped himself up on one elbow and used his other hand to cup one side of her face. 'You've gone very quiet.' His gaze held hers in an intimate lock she found hard to hold. 'I hope it's a good quiet, not a bad quiet.'

She lowered her gaze to his mouth and gave a flickering smile. 'It's not often in my life that I become speechless.'

He tipped up her chin to mesh his gaze with hers. 'Same.' His thumb brushed over her lower lip in a slow caress that made her whole mouth tingle. 'You're breathtaking, do you know that?' His voice had a husky edge and his eyes darkened to pitch. 'No one has ever got under my skin quite as much as you.'

'Good to know I'm not the only one who feels like that,' Zoey said, gently caressing his strong jaw. 'But, given this is just a fling, I think we need to be careful we don't start confusing good sex with something else.'

'I'm not confused, but are you?' His tone was playful but there was a faint disturbance at the back of his gaze. A shifting shadow, fleeting, furtive.

Zoey stretched her lips into a confident smile. 'Not so far.'

His eyes moved back and forth between hers as if he was looking for something. 'Better keep it that way, babe. I don't want to hurt you.' There was a roughened edge in his voice. 'That's the last thing I want to do.'

'Ah, but I might be the one who ends up hurting you,' Zoey countered in a teasing tone. 'Have you considered that?'

There was another tiny flicker at the back of his gaze but then his expression became inscrutable. 'I guess I'll have to take my chances.' And he sealed her mouth with his.

CHAPTER NINE

LATER THAT EVENING, Finn brought a bottle of champagne and a cheese and fruit board out to the terrace overlooking the sparkling lights of Monte Carlo and the moonlit sea in the distance. Zoey was leaning against the stone balustrade, her long, dark hair lustrous around her shoulders, her face turned towards the golden orb of the moon. She was wearing a long white shoestring-strap sundress that showcased every delicious curve of her body. He wondered if he would ever get tired of looking at her. His pulse leapt every time he came near her, the memory of their lovemaking stirring his blood anew.

The rattle of the glasses on the tray he was carrying alerted her to his presence and she turned round and smiled, and something in his chest stung like the sudden flick of a rubber band. Maybe it was the moonlight, maybe it was the passionate lovemaking earlier…or maybe it was a warning he needed to rein it in a little.

Her comment earlier about the possibility of her hurting him would have been laughable if anyone else had said it. He never allowed anyone close enough to give them the power to hurt him.

But Zoey was getting close, a little too close for comfort.

She knew him intimately, far more intimately than any other lover. And that intimate physical knowledge had somehow given her the uncanny ability to tempt him into lowering his guard. He had brought her away to spend concentrated time with her because he wanted continuity rather than having one night here and one night there.

Having her to himself, day upon day, night upon night, had deepened his desire for her and also made him appreciate how talented she was and how she hadn't been given a proper chance to shine. He had a plan for her irrespective of the timeframe of their fling—he wanted her on his creative team going forward. He didn't want her to disappear out of his life once their fling was over. Whether she would agree to it was another question, but he would make her an attractive offer, one she would be a fool to refuse.

A part of him was a little disquieted about the lengths to which he was prepared to go in order to keep her. He normally kept his emotions out of business. He hadn't built his empire by being swayed by his feelings but by concentrating on the facts. But the fact was, Zoey was a one in a million person and he didn't want to lose her to someone else. She would be an asset to his business and, since his business was his main priority, he would do anything to keep her. Almost anything.

'Ooh, lovely, a moonlit champagne supper,' Zoey said. 'You really know how to spoil a girl. But then, you've had plenty of practice.'

'Some women are harder to impress than others,' Finn said. 'But worth the effort in the end.'

'And which category am I in?'

'You're in a category of your own.'

Zoey was the first woman he had brought here, and right now he couldn't imagine bringing anyone else. It would seem…odd, tacky…almost clichéd. He knew it was how she saw him. As some well-practised charmer who slept his way through droves of lovers. And there was some uncomfortable truth in her view of him. That was the way he lived his life and he would no doubt go back to that lifestyle once their fling was over.

Finn frowned as he placed the tray on the table and took the champagne out of the ice bucket. The kicker was, what if he didn't want it to be over any time soon? What if Zoey wanted to end it before he did? What if the possibility of her hurting him became a painful, inescapable reality? What if that little elastic band flick in his chest became a thousand flicks? Ten thousand? More?

'Is something wrong?' Zoey asked, catching the tail end of his frown.

Finn gave a crooked smile. 'What could be wrong? I've got the most beautiful woman with me on a perfect night in Monte Carlo.'

Her gaze slipped away from his and her hand left his arm to scoop her hair back behind one shoulder. 'I guess I'm just one of many you've brought here.' She walked back over to the balustrade and stood with her back to him, her slim shoulders going down on a sigh.

Finn put the champagne bottle back in the ice bucket and came over to her. He placed his hands on the tops of her shoulders and turned her to face him. 'You're the first person I've brought here.'

Doubt flickered in her violet gaze. 'I find that hard to believe, given your reputation.'

'It's true, Zoey. I've only just had the renovations done and there hasn't been time to entertain a guest before now.'

'But you'll bring others here once our fling is over.'

Finn removed his hands from her shoulders and frowned. 'Is that a crime?'

'No.' She gave a stiff little smile and added, 'I'll have other lovers too.'

The sting in his chest was not the flick of a rubber band this time but a whip. Finn walked back to open the champagne, a frown pulling at his forehead. He wasn't a card-carrying member of the double standards club, but right now he was having trouble handling the thought of her making love with anyone else. He pulled the cork of the champagne with a loud pop and poured some in each of the glasses, but he had never felt less like drinking it. He brought the glasses over to where she was standing and offered her one.

She took it with another smile and then clinked her glass against his. 'Let's hope my future lovers are as exciting as you.'

Finn put his glass down on the edge of the balustrade without taking a sip. 'For God's sake, Zoey,' he said with a savage frown.

She arched her eyebrows in an imperious manner. 'What? You're being a little touchy, are you not? I'm simply stating a fact. We'll both go back to our normal lives once we end our relationship. In fact, you've done me a favour in breaking my self-imposed man drought. I haven't been with anyone since I broke up with my ex and wondered if I would ever take a lover again. But you've helped me get back in the dating game.'

He scraped a hand through his hair and muttered a curse not quite under his breath. 'Glad to be of service.'

'Why should the mention of my future lovers be an issue for you? You'll probably have dozens after me, hundreds even.'

One thing Finn knew for sure—none of them would be half as exciting as her. 'I'm not sure you'll find the casual dating scene as fulfilling as you think.'

'Does that mean you don't find it so?'

Finn hadn't found it so for months but wasn't going to admit it to anyone. He was barely ready to admit it to himself. Admitting it to himself would mean he would need to change how he lived his life, and he wasn't sure he wanted to explore the possibility of doing that in any great detail. He was used to being alone, apart from brief flings. He was used to being self-sufficient. He was used to having the control to start or end a relationship on his terms. Sharing that control with another person was in the too-hard, too-threatening basket.

Finn took one of her hands and brought it up to his chest. 'I don't want to think about you with anyone else, not while we're having such a good time.' He gave her hand a gentle squeeze. 'You're having a good time, yes?'

Her lips curved in a smile. 'I can't remember when I've enjoyed myself more.'

Finn placed his arms around her and gathered her close, resting his head on the top of her head. 'Nor me.'

The next few days were some of the most memorable of Zoey's life. They spent considerable time in

Nice, looking at the hotel Leo Frascatelli was currently redeveloping. The hotel was situated close to the sweeping arc of the beach and had various restaurants and bars that made the most of the spectacular view. It was in the process of extensive renovations, which were now close to being completed, to coincide with the launch of the advertising campaign.

On another day they toured the ancient fortress town of St Paul de Vence, high up in the hills behind Nice, strolling hand in hand up and down the narrow cobblestoned alleys, wandering in and out of the galleries and artisan shops. They went to the renowned perfume village of Grasse, where Finn bought her some gorgeous fragrances to take home. They had a leisurely lunch in the resort town of Cannes, famous for its international film festival, and then visited the ancient market place in Antibes, and gazed at the jaw-droppingly expensive yachts moored in the port.

Being in Finn's company every hour of the day, whether they were sightseeing, working or dining or making love, made Zoey realise how dangerously close she was to falling in love with him. He treated her like a princess and yet still managed to make her feel his equal in every way. He was tender and caring, looking at her with such focussed concentration at times, she began to wonder if he was developing a stronger attachment to her than he was prepared to admit.

And, unless she was seriously deluding herself, she had seen that same look on her friends' fiancés' faces. A look so tender and caring it made her blood sing with joy. Every time she tried to imagine a future without him, a wave of dread swept through her. He was an attentive and considerate and exciting lover and, as much as she had teased him over one day moving on to other lovers, she was beginning to realise it would be near impossible for her to do so without disappointment. Acute, heart-wrenching disappointment. For who could possibly compare to him and his exquisite lovemaking?

But it wasn't just his lovemaking she would miss. She enjoyed listening to his insights into the advertising business. She felt inspired by his work ethic and stamina. And, while he was a hard task master when they were working together on their creative approach to the Frascatelli account, she found herself rising to the challenge, enjoying the repartee and exchange of ideas. He encouraged her to be bold in her vision, bolder than she had ever been, and it freed her to explore and stretch her creativity in a way she had never done before.

But a tiny seed of doubt kept rattling around her brain over her future working for him. Becoming one of his employees was not the same as owning and operating her own business. How could she operate in a business that was no longer hers?

But, then it had never been hers—her father had seen to that.

The takeover would take some weeks to finally settle, in terms of which staff would be let go and which would move across to Finn's company. Could she work with him in the long term once their fling was over? How would it feel to see him every day but not in their current context? He would go back to his playboy lifestyle and she would have to learn to be indifferent to him. Indifferent to the many women who came and went in his life. She would have to pretend it didn't bother her, pretend he didn't matter to her other than as an employer.

But he did matter.

He mattered more than she wanted to admit. But it was beyond foolish to hope she might matter to him too.

On their last night in Monte Carlo, Finn took Zoey to a restaurant near the Monte Carlo casino and the stunning Hotel de Paris. They were seated at their table with drinks in front of them, waiting for their meals to arrive. He had been quieter than normal for most of the day and she hadn't been game enough to ask why. Over the last few hours, she'd often found him looking into the distance with a slight frown on his face.

Was he thinking of ending their fling now they'd had this concentrated time together? His flings were notoriously short—some only lasted a day or two. What right did she have to hope he would want her for longer? That he might have come to care for her the same way she had come to care for him?

Care? What a mild word to use when what she felt for him was much stronger, much deeper, much more lasting.

Much more terrifying.

Love was a word she had never thought to use when it came to Finn O'Connell. But now it was the only word she could use to describe how she felt about him. It wasn't a simple, friendship love, although she did consider him more of a friend now than an enemy. It was an all-consuming love that had sprouted and blossomed over the last few days, maybe even before that. The first time they made love had triggered a change in her attitude towards him, and not just because of the explosively passionate sex. The union of their bodies had triggered a union of their minds, their interests, their talents and even their disappointments about some aspects of their childhoods. Zoey had sensed an emotional camaraderie with him she had not felt with anyone else.

Was it silly of her to hope he felt the same way? That he would want to continue their fling…maybe even call it a relationship rather than a fling and one day allow it to become permanent?

How had she fooled herself that she never wanted to settle down? She wasn't cut out for the single-and-loving-it club. She longed for deep and lasting love, a love that could help overcome the trials and tribulations of life. A love that was a true partnership, a commitment of two equals working together to build a happy and productive life. A family life where children were welcomed, loved, supported and encouraged to grow and be all they could and wanted to be. Zoey had denied those longings until she'd met Finn, but now those deep yearnings were not to be so easily ignored.

Finn reached for her hand across the table, his fingers warm around hers. The candle on the table reflected light back into his dark brown eyes and cast parts of his face in shadow, as though he were a Gothic hero. How could she have thought she wouldn't fall in love with him? How could she have thought she would be immune to his charismatic presence, his admirable qualities, his earth-shattering lovemaking? He was everything she wanted in a life partner but had never thought to find. It wasn't enough to have him as a temporary lover. How could she ever have thought a fling with him would quell the need he evoked in her?

Zoey looked down at their joined hands, his touch so familiar and yet still as electrifying. She glanced up to meet his gaze and found him looking at her with unusual intensity.

'There's something I want to run by you.' His voice was low-pitched and husky.

Zoey disguised a swallow, her heart giving a tiny leap in her chest. Could her nascent hopes be realised after all? Did he want to extend their fling, to make it a little more permanent? 'Yes?'

There was a moment or two of silence. His gaze slowly roved over her face, as if he were memorising her features one by one. His thumb began to stroke the fleshy part of her thumb and a shiver coursed down her spine. His gaze finally steadied on hers. Dark…enigmatically dark. 'How do you feel about becoming my partner?'

His partner? Zoey blinked, as if a too bright a light had shone in her eyes. Her heart jumped. Her stomach flip-flopped. Her pulse tripped and began to sprint. 'Y-your partner?' Her voice stumbled over the word, her thoughts flying every which way like a flock of startled birds.

Surely he didn't mean…? Was he proposing to her? No, surely not? He would be more direct if he was proposing marriage, wouldn't he? Should she ask? No, definitely not. Her heart began to thump so loudly she could hear its echo in her ears, feel its punch against her ribcage. 'I—I don't quite understand…'

'My business partner.' His mouth slanted in a smile. 'I don't just want you to come and work for me, I want you to work with me—alongside me. These last few days have shown how we work brilliantly together and how we balance each other so well. I know we'll make a great creative team.'

A great creative team… He was offering her a stake in his business, not in his personal life. Her heart sank. He was talking business, but she was hoping for happy-ever-after. How could she have thought it would be anything else? Zoey pulled her hand out of his before he felt it trembling against his. Her whole body was beginning to tremble, not with excitement but an inexplicable pang of disappointment. She gave herself a hard mental slap. How could she have thought he was going to propose *marriage* to her? He wasn't the marrying type. She had fooled herself into thinking those tender looks he'd been giving her meant something more. How could she have been such an idiot?

He was offering her a dream—a different dream.

A dream career, working with him in one of the most successful agencies in the world.

A business partnership.

Not the dream partnership she most wanted—a lifelong partnership of love and commitment.

'Wow… I'll have to think about it for a day or two…' Zoey gave a fractured laugh and added, 'For a moment there, I thought you were proposing something else.'

There was a thick beat of silence.

'I hope you weren't unduly disappointed?' His gaze was marksman-steady, but the rest of his expression was inscrutable.

Zoey picked up her wine glass to do something with her hands. She kept her features under strict control. No way would she show him how disappointed she was. She had way too much pride for that. He had always been upfront about his level of commitment. She was the one who had gone off-script and begun wishing for the moon and the stars and the rarest of comets too. She was the one who had deluded herself into thinking they had a future together. Finn had never promised a future, only a fling. 'Why would I be disappointed?'

'Why indeed?'

She took a generous sip of wine and kept the glass in her hands, watching one of her fingers smoothing away the condensation marks on the side. 'You seem to have come to this decision rather quickly.' She glanced at him again. 'I mean, there must be other people you've considered letting into the business before now?'

'No one quite like you.'

Zoey looked at the contents of her glass again.

'I'm hugely flattered. More than a little gobsmacked, actually.' She gave another cracked laugh. 'I've been working alongside my father for ten years and he never once offered me a directorship. I've only been sleeping with you for just over a week and you're offering me a dream proposition.'

'This has nothing to do with us sleeping together.' His tone was adamant, his expression flickering with sudden tension.

Zoey raised her eyebrows and forced herself to hold his gaze. 'Doesn't it?'

Finn sat back in his chair and picked up his wine glass. 'This is strictly a business decision. You're extremely talented and haven't yet had that talent properly tapped. You will bring to the company new energy and innovation. I have a good creative team but with you on board it will be brilliant.' He took a sip of wine and put his glass back down, his eyes holding hers and added, 'Besides, I don't want to lose you to someone else.'

He didn't want to lose her. If only he meant those words the way she wanted him to. Zoey ran the tip of her tongue over her dry lips. 'It's certainly a wonderful opportunity. But will my name be on the company letterhead or just yours?'

'Come on, Zoey, you know about branding better than most,' he said with a frown. 'I've spent years building my company's name and reputation. I'm not going to change it now. The deal I'm offering you is generous enough without that.' He named a sum that sent her eyebrows up again. 'How does that sound?'

'It sounds almost impossible to resist.' Just like he was, which was why she needed more time before she signed on the dotted line. 'But I'd still like a day or two to think it over.'

'Fine. But don't take too long. I want to get things on the move as quickly as possible.'

'I understand, but a lot has happened in a short time,' Zoey said. 'The takeover, us getting involved, now this. It's a lot for me to process.'

Finn reached for her hand again. 'Your father was a fool not to allow you more control in his company. If he had given you more creative freedom, then he wouldn't have felt the need to sell to me.'

'It would have been nice if I'd been involved in the process.'

'I'm involving you now.'

Zoey couldn't hold his gaze and stared at her wine instead. 'What if he doesn't stop drinking even though he's no longer running the company?'

Finn placed his hand over hers. 'Look at me.'

She lifted her gaze with a sigh. 'I can't help worrying about him.'

He stroked the back of her hand with his thumb. 'He's not your responsibility. If he doesn't choose to get the help he clearly needs, then it won't be your fault. You have to step back and let him face the consequences of his choices. There's no other way.'

Zoey knew he was right, but the knowing and the doing were as far apart as two sides of a giant chasm. 'He's the only link I have left to my mother. The only person I can ask about her to keep my fading memories of her alive.'

'Tell me about her. What was she like?' His tone was gentle, his gaze equally so.

Zoey gave a wistful smile. 'She was funny and a bit wild at times.'

'Now, why doesn't that surprise me?' His tone was dry.

She smothered a soft laugh and continued, 'She loved to cook, and she made Christmas and birthdays so special.' Her smile faded, her shoulders dropping down on a sigh. 'I missed her so much. I still miss her. She left a hole in my life that nothing and no one can ever fill. I don't think I've ever felt as loved by anyone else.'

'Not even by your father?'

Zoey rolled her eyes. 'No.'

'What about before your mum died? Did you feel loved by him then?'

Zoey thought about it before answering, casting her mind back to the early years before tragedy had so cruelly struck. 'It's funny you should ask that… I've never really thought about this before, but he was a lot warmer to me back then. He wasn't as physically demonstrative as my mum was, but I don't remember feeling like he didn't love me. I'm a bit like him in that I'm not comfortable with showing physical affection.'

'You could have fooled me.'

Zoey could feel her cheeks warming. 'Yes, well, I did tell you, you have a very strange effect on me.'

'Likewise.' His eyes glinted.

She looked down at their joined hands and returned the caress by stroking the strong, corded tendons on the back of his hand. A shiver passed over her at the thought of the pleasure his hands gave her, the pleasure that thrummed in her flesh even now like a plucked cello string.

Why had she thought she could keep her emotions out of a fling with him? Her emotions had been engaged right from the start. 'Losing my mother changed everything between my father and me. It was like the bottom fell out of our world that day. I know it certainly fell out of mine.' She glanced up at him and gave a twisted smile. 'I still see my stepmothers. I haven't told my father, though. He doesn't part with his exes on good terms. But they were each good to me in their own way and I missed having them around—especially the last one, Linda. She's a lot like my mother, actually.'

'Maybe your father was worried about losing

you too,' Finn said. 'It can happen after a sudden loss. People become terrified it might happen to someone else they love, so they tone down how they feel to protect themselves.'

Zoey wondered if Finn had done the same after his parents had chosen their drinking and drugs lifestyle over him. 'You could be right, I suppose, but I'm not riding my hopes on it. I'm twenty-eight years old. I don't need to hear my father say he loves me every day.'

'But it would be nice if he showed it in some way.' Finn's hand squeezed hers, his gaze holding hers in an intimate tether that made something warm flow down her spine.

'Yes...'

Finn released her hand and signalled to the waiter for the bill. 'We'd better have an early night. We have a lot of work to do when we get home to London.'

Later that night, Finn reached for Zoey in the dark, drawing her close to his side. He breathed in the scent of her hair, his blood stirring as she nestled into him with a sigh. Their lovemaking earlier had been as passionate as always, but something had changed—or maybe he had changed. It hadn't felt as basic as smoking-hot sex between two consenting adults but a mutual worship of each other's bodies. He began to wonder if he would find anyone else who so perfectly suited him in bed. Their lovemaking got better and better, the pleasure, the intensity, the depth of feeling—all of it made him realise how shallow and how solely body-based his other encounters had been.

Zoey was not just a convenient body to have sex with—not merely yet another consenting adult to have a good time with then say goodbye to and never think of again. He wondered if there would be a time when he wouldn't think of her. She filled his thoughts to the exclusion of everything else.

Finn had never been much of a fan of sleepovers in the past. The morning-after routine got a little tiresome, the attraction of the night before fading to the point where he often couldn't wait to get away. But with Zoey it was completely different. He enjoyed waking up beside her each day, enjoyed the feel of her body against him, enjoyed seeing her sleepy smile and feeling her arms go round him.

But he was surprised she hadn't jumped at his offer of a business relationship last night over dinner. Surprised and disappointed she hadn't been as enthusiastic as he'd hoped. It was a big step for him to take and one he had never taken before. He had run his company singlehandedly from the get-go and had resisted bringing anyone else on board. But he knew Zoey's gifts and talents would be an asset to him and he couldn't allow her to take them elsewhere. He was impatient for her answer so he could get things in motion. There were legal things to see to, paperwork to draw up, contracts to sign—all of it would take time. He had pushed their flight back a couple of hours, determined to get her answer before they went home to London.

Zoey snuggled against him and opened one sleepy eye. 'Is it time to get up yet?'

'Not yet. I delayed our flights a couple of hours.'

She rolled onto her tummy, her slim legs entwined with his. She traced a slow circle around his mouth, making his lips tingle. 'Oh? Why? So we can loll about in bed all morning?'

Finn captured her hand and held it against his chest. 'I want your answer. Today. Before we fly back to London.' He didn't want to waste any more time. He had to know one way or the other.

Her hand fell away from his face and her expression clouded. 'I told you I need to think about it. There's a lot to consider.' She moved away from him and, throwing back the doona, got off the bed, wrapping herself in her satin bathrobe and tying the waist ties.

'Like what?' Finn frowned, rising from the bed as well. He picked up his trousers and stepped into them. 'I'm offering you an amazing opportunity. What's taking you so long to decide?'

Zoey turned away. 'I don't want to talk about it now. Stop pressuring me.'

Finn came up behind her and took her by the

shoulders and turned her to face him. 'But I want to talk about it now.'

Her chin came up and a stubborn light shone in her eyes. 'Okay, we'll talk, but you might not want to hear what I have to say.'

'Try me.' He removed his hands from her shoulders, locking his gaze on hers.

She drew in a deep breath and let it out in a steady stream. 'What you're offering me is an extremely generous offer. Hugely generous. But it's not enough. I want more. Much more.'

Finn choked back an incredulous laugh. 'Not enough? Then I'll double it.'

Her gaze continued to hold his with unnerving intensity. 'I'm not talking about the money, Finn.'

He looked at her blankly for a moment. If it wasn't about money, then what was it about? 'Since when is a business deal not about money?'

'I don't just want to be your partner in business.'

A prickly sensation crawled across his scalp. 'Then what do you want?'

Twin pools of colour formed in her cheeks, but her eyes lost none of their unwavering focus. 'I want to be someone important to you.'

'You *are* important to me,' Finn said. 'I've offered you a deal that would be the envy of most people in our field.'

'But why did you offer it to me?'

'I told you before—I don't want to lose you.' He

scraped a hand through his hair and added, 'You'll be a valuable asset to me.'

A hard look came into her eyes. 'And what happens once our fling is over? Will I still be an asset to you then?'

'Of course. Our involvement ending doesn't change that. Why should it? This is purely a business decision.'

She gave a hollow laugh, her expression cynical. 'You still don't get it, do you? You talk about your business decisions, but you won't talk about your feelings.'

'Okay, I'll talk about my feelings,' Finn said. 'I feel insulted you aren't jumping at the chance to come on board with me. You complain about spending years pushed to the sidelines by your father, with your talent withering on the vine, and here I am offering you a deal to die for and you're deliberating.'

Zoey walked a little further away, her arms going across her body. 'I don't think I can work with you once our fling is over. It will be too… awkward.'

'Why? We're both mature adults, Zoey. We're not teenagers who can't regulate their emotions.'

She flicked him a glance over her shoulder. 'I think it's best if we end it now before it gets any more complicated.'

Finn stared at her for a speechless moment. End

it? Now? The prickly sensation on his scalp moved down the length of his spine and down the backs of his legs. He wanted to move towards her but couldn't get his legs to work. He wanted to insist she change her mind, to beg her to reconsider…but then he realised he would be demeaning himself in pleading with her to stay with him.

His days of begging and pleading with anyone were well and truly over.

'Okay, we'll end it if that's what you want,' Finn said, trying not to think about what that would look like, how it would feel to see her and not be involved with her. 'But the directorship offer is still on the table.'

Zoey turned to face him, her expression difficult to read. 'I can't accept it, Finn. I can't work with you.'

He frowned so hard his forehead hurt. 'You work brilliantly with me. Hasn't the last few days shown you that? We make a great team, Zoey, you know we do. Why would you walk away from that?'

'I'll call Leo Frascatelli and tell him I'm handing the account over to you,' Zoey said. 'I'll find another job somewhere and—'

'Do you want me to beg? Is that what you want?' Finn said through tight lips. Never had he felt so out of balance. So out of kilter. So desperate, and yet so desperate not to show it. Emotions he didn't know he possessed reared up inside him, clamouring for an outlet. Hurt, grief, despair… loneliness at the thought of losing her. Of not seeing her every day, of not making love to her.

'No, Finn, what I want is for you to feel about me the way I feel about you.'

Finn approached her and, unpeeling her arms from around her body, took her hands in his. He searched her face for a moment, his thoughts in a tangled knot. 'Are you saying you…?' He didn't want to say the word because he couldn't say it back. He had never told anyone he loved them, not since he was a child. And look how his love had been rewarded back then—with abandonment. Brutal abandonment. Loving someone to that degree gave them the power to hurt you, to leave you, to destroy you.

'I used to think I hated you,' Zoey said. 'But, after getting to know you more, I realised I was actually quite similar to you in some ways. That's why I was so confident I could have a fling with you without involving my feelings—but I was wrong, so very wrong.'

'Zoey…' He took an unsteady breath. 'Look, you know I care about you. I enjoy being with you. But I'm not willing to commit to anything more. We agreed on the terms—a fling for as long as we both wanted it.'

'But I don't want it now.' She pulled out of his

hold and stepped back. 'There's no point continuing a relationship that isn't working for me.'

'How is it not working?' Finn asked. 'We've just spent five wonderful days together and you say it's not working?'

'I'm not talking about the sex. It's been perfect in every way, but one day that will come to an end, because that's how your casual flings work. You don't commit in the long-term, you don't want it to be for ever. But casual and uncommitted isn't enough for me any more. I can't be with you knowing you'll end it when someone else catches your attention.'

No one had captured Finn's attention like Zoey. No one. And he wondered if they ever would. But she was asking too much. Long-term commitment wasn't in his skill set. He no longer had the commitment gene. He had erased it from his system. He didn't want to feel so deeply about someone that he would promise to spend the rest of his days with them, always wondering if they would walk away without a backward glance. He strode away a couple of steps, his hand rubbing at the corded tension in the back of his neck.

'What did you think I was proposing last night over dinner?' He gave a bark of cynical laughter. 'Marriage?'

Zoey let out a long sigh. 'You know, I did for a moment think you were considering something a little longer term between us. You've been so wonderful to me over the last few days, so attentive and, yes, loving, even if you don't want to call it by that name. I wondered if you were falling in love with me, rather than just being in lust with me.'

'Marriage was never and will never be on the table.'

'Which is why we have to end this now. I want for ever, Finn. Is it unreasonable to want someone to love me for a lifetime? I want a man to commit solely to me. To love me and treasure me, not just as a sexual partner but as a life partner. I want a partner in life, not just a partner in bed or in business.'

'The latter two are the only ones I can offer. Take it or leave it.'

Zoey hugged her arms around her body. 'You told me a while back when we were talking about my dad it was pointless to expect someone to change if they weren't capable of it. So, I'm going to take your advice—I'm not going to waste any more of my life hoping you'll change because I'll get even more hurt in the end.'

How like her to throw his own words back at him, Finn thought. Words he had lived by for years and which he'd found perfectly reasonable. But now they contained an irony that cut to the quick. Stinging him in a way he never expected to be stung. He was losing her on both counts—

she wanted to end their fling and she was rejecting his business proposal.

It was a novel experience for him, being on the other end of a break-up. The one who was left, not the one who was doing the leaving. That hadn't happened since he'd been a kid. But he refused to show her how much it affected him, how much it disappointed and riled him to have the tables turned. 'If you want to end our involvement, then end it. But you're making a big mistake in walking away from the chance to be in business with me. I won't be offering it again if you suddenly change your mind.'

The determined light came back into her eyes. 'I won't change my mind.' She turned and began to gather her things together.

'What are you doing?'

'I'm packing. I'll make my own way back to London.'

'Don't be ridiculous, Zoey,' Finn said. 'There's no need for such histrionics. I've booked our flight for eleven a.m. You don't need to rush off now.'

She folded an article of clothing and held it against her stomach. 'I think it's best we make a clean break of things, starting now.'

He wanted to stop her. To convince her to rethink her decision, to have just a few more hours with her before they went their separate ways. But the words were stuck in the back of his throat, blocked behind a wall of pride. 'Have it your way, then.'

Finn shrugged himself into a shirt and shoved his feet into his shoes and made his way to the door.

'Aren't you going to say goodbye?' Zoey asked.

Finn gave her a cutting look. 'I just did.' And he walked out and closed the door behind him with a resounding click.

Zoey bit down on her lower lip until she thought it would bleed. How could she have thought it would be any different between them? Finn was never going to change, just like her ex had refused to change. And she would be a fool to live in hope Finn would one day develop feelings for her. How many years would she have to wait? One? Two? Seven? Ten?

It was better this way, better for her to make a new start, to put her lost hopes and dreams behind her and forge her own way forward.

Finn was angry at her for not accepting his offer but that came out of his arrogance in believing she couldn't resist any terms he presented her. She could resist. She had to resist, otherwise she would be reverting to old habits. Her old self had toed the line, adapted, lived in hope but been too afraid to embrace her own agency. Too afraid to voice her needs and instead had kept them locked inside.

But Zoey was no longer that person. She had morphed into a person who took charge of her own destiny, who openly stated her needs and was prepared to live with the consequences if they failed to be met. She would no longer stay with a man in the hope of happy-ever-after. And certainly not a man like Finn who didn't even believe in the concept of a once-in-a-lifetime love.

Zoey packed and was out the door and in a taxi within half an hour. It was no surprise Finn didn't return to the villa and try and beg her to change her mind, but she was heartbroken all the same. All her life she had yearned to be loved, to be treasured and valued, and now she had been denied it yet again. By the one man with whom she thought she could be truly happy.

'You were right,' Zoey said to Ivy and Millie a few days later when they caught up for coffee. 'I fell in love with Finn.'

Ivy and Millie leaned forward in their chairs. 'And?' They spoke in unison, hopeful expressions on their faces.

Zoey shook her head and sighed. 'And nothing. I broke things off.'

'Oh, hon, I'm so sorry,' Ivy said. 'What happened?'

'He doesn't feel the same way and I was too stupid to realise it. I thought he was about to propose to me over dinner on our last night in Monte Carlo but he was only offering me a business deal.'

Millie's eyes rounded. 'A business deal? Oh,

Zoey, I really feel for you. Under different circumstances that would have been so good. I don't suppose you accepted?'

Zoey screwed up her face. 'I can't possibly work with him now. Can you imagine how hard it would be to see him every day? To hear other staff talking about his latest squeeze in the tea room?' She picked up her latte from the table in front of them. 'I'm looking for a job elsewhere.'

'But what about the account you were working on with him?' Millie asked. 'The Frasca whatsit?'

'Frascatelli,' Zoey said. 'I forfeited it to Finn.'

'I know how upsetting it is to be in your position—we both do, don't we, Millie? But was that wise?' Ivy asked. 'You wanted that project so badly.'

'Maybe not wise, but necessary,' Zoey said with another sigh. 'I never thought I'd fall for anyone the way I've fallen for Finn. He's the only man I could ever imagine spending the rest of my life with but he's dead set against commitment.'

'But he committed to you during your fling, didn't he?' Millie asked. 'I mean, it was exclusive between you, wasn't it?'

'Yes, I insisted on that,' Zoey said. 'And, what's more, I trusted him implicitly.'

'Well, it shows he can commit,' Ivy put in. 'But maybe he needs more time to realise what he feels for you. You've had a bit of a whirlwind affair.

Maybe he hasn't yet come to terms with how he feels. Commitment-shy men can be a bit slow to realise how they feel.'

But how long would she have to wait? Years, as she'd waited for her father to change? She was done with waiting, wishing and hoping for change. 'Finn treated me with the utmost respect and consideration. I know this sounds strange, but I *felt* like he was growing to love me, you know? That's why I thought he was going to pop the question. God, I feel like such an idiot now.' She groaned. 'How can a man make love to you so beautifully and not care about you in some way?'

'I wish I could say it will all work out in the end like it did for Millie and I,' Ivy said. 'But that's probably not all that helpful to you now, while you're hurting so much.'

'Has he contacted you since you came back from Monte Carlo?' Millie asked.

'A text message to inform me of the meetings he's having with the Brackenfield staff,' Zoey said. 'No doubt he's going to fire half of them and not feel even a twinge of conscience about it.'

'The deal Finn offered you,' Millie said. 'Surely he wouldn't have offered it to you unless he didn't think you'd be an asset to the company? It's a huge compliment to you. I just wonder if you're being a bit hasty in rejecting it out of hand.'

'But he only wants me to be an invisible director,' Zoey said. 'My name won't be on the letterhead—he told me so. I've worked for ten years for the Brackenfield name and now it's going to completely disappear, swallowed up by him.'

'You can't talk him into a compromise?' Millie ventured.

Zoey drained her coffee before answering. 'Finn O'Connell doesn't know the meaning of the word.' And her days of compromising were well and truly over.

Zoey called in on her father on her way back from coffee with the girls to find him halfway through a bottle of wine. And it wasn't his first. There was an empty bottle on the bench.

He held up a glass, swaying slightly on his feet. 'Have a drink to celebrate my retirement.'

'Dad, I'm not here to celebrate anything,' Zoey said. 'I'm here to tell you I won't see you again unless the next time it's in a rehab clinic. Your choice—the drink or me.'

He frowned, as if he couldn't process what she was saying. He scratched his head and frowned. 'But you always visit me.'

'I know, and it's going to stop,' Zoey said. 'For years I've visited you, I've had countless lunches or dinners with you, I cover for you, I make excuses for you—and what have I got in return? You continue to drink and embarrass me. Not only that, you sold out on me to Finn O'Connell. I waited for years for you to promote me, to allow me to reach my potential, but you never did. Why am I so unimportant to you?'

He put the glass down, a frown still wrinkling his brow. 'You're not unimportant…'

'But the drink is more important,' Zoey said. 'You wanted a son. You've made no secret of that and instead you got me. And I tried to be the best daughter I could be but it's not enough. I'm not enough for you.' Just as she hadn't been enough for her ex. And as she wasn't enough for Finn, and how that hurt way more than anything.

'You are enough for me…' Her father looked at her with bloodshot eyes, his voice trembling. 'When I lost your mother…' His hand shook as he rubbed at his unshaven face. 'I kept thinking I might lose you too. I—I found it hard to be close to you after that. I seem to lose everyone I care about. I know I always carry on about wanting a son but that was the way I was brought up. A son to carry on the family name was my dream, but when your mother died, well, that dream was shattered. And when Linda left me a few months ago I began to drink to numb my feelings. I lost interest in everything. Work was just a burden. I couldn't wait to offload the company.'

So, Finn had been right about her father, Zoey thought. He had told her that her dad was most likely protecting himself from further hurt after losing her mother. Was that what Finn was doing too? Protecting himself after the rejection of his parents' love? Strange that he would have such insight into her father but not have it into himself. Or maybe he did have it but just didn't love her. She had been a convenient fling partner but not someone he loved enough to spend the rest of his life with her in marriage.

'Will you promise to get help?' Zoey asked her father, determined not to back down.

He gave a stuttering sigh. 'I've made promises before and never kept them…' He winced as if in deep pain and added, 'But if it means losing you…'

Tears began to roll down his face and Zoey went to him and hugged him, fighting tears herself.

It would be a long journey but at least her father had taken the first painful step.

CHAPTER TEN

FINN IMMERSED HIMSELF in work over the next four weeks to distract himself from Zoey's decision to end their fling. But the endless meetings with the Brackenfield staff were a constant reminder of her. He found it hard to decide on who to keep and who to let go. His emotions kept getting in the way.

Yes, his emotions, those pesky things he never allowed anywhere near a business decision. He offered generous redundancy packages to some, far more generous than they probably deserved. But he kept thinking of Zoey, how she saw the staff as people beyond their desks, people with families and loved ones and worries and stresses to deal with in their personal lives.

But he had his own stress to deal with in his personal life—the stress of missing Zoey.

He missed everything about her—her smile, her laughter, her feistiness when she didn't agree with him on something, her touch, her kisses, the explosive way she responded to his lovemaking. There was a constant ache in his chest, a dragging ache that distracted him during the day and kept him awake at night. He had never reacted to a break-up so badly. But then, he had always been the instigator of his previous break-ups with casual lovers. He never allowed anyone the power to hurt him, to abandon him—he always got in first. Was that why his break-up with Zoey was so hard to handle? He hadn't seen her as a casual lover—she was in a completely different category, but he wasn't exactly sure what it was.

Finn hadn't even thought of taking another lover. His stomach turned at the thought. So much for his playboy lifestyle. He was turning into a monk. A miserably lonely monk. He spent most evenings with only his one-eyed cat for company.

Finn felt a strange sense of camaraderie with his battered and brooding cat. Tolstoy had been hurt in the past and went out of his way to avoid further hurt. That was why, when Finn had gone away to New York and then Monte Carlo, Tolstoy had punished him on his return. Fear was behind that behaviour, fear of being permanently rejected. But, since Finn had been home every evening over the last month, Tolstoy had built up enough trust to lose some of his guardedness. It occurred to him then that Tolstoy loved him and was terrified he might not come back.

Why hadn't he realised that before now?

Maybe it wasn't Finn's dented pride that was causing this infernal pain in his chest. Maybe he was a little more like his cat than he realised. Didn't they say pets and owners became alike? Finn didn't like to think of himself as the sort of man who couldn't move on after a woman had ended a fling. He knew how to let go—he'd been doing it without a problem for years.

But this didn't feel like a cut and dried case of injured male pride.

It felt like something else…something he had never felt before…something that was threatening the entire basis on which he lived his footloose and fancy-free life. Something beyond a fleeing attraction…something deeper—a sense that if he never saw Zoey again he would be missing something essential to his existence. Without her, he would not be the person he was meant to be. He would be stunted in some way, reduced, lacking. She inspired him, enthralled him, delighted and fulfilled him.

Zoey hadn't said the words 'I love you' out loud but she had told him she had developed feelings for him. Feelings that had grown from negative to positive. Feelings he had rebuffed out of fear. Why hadn't he seen that until now? He was as one-eyed as his cat not to have seen it. He'd been afraid to love her in case he lost her and yet he had lost her anyway. He had spent his whole life avoiding love, avoiding emotional attachment in case he was rejected. But he had rejected the most amazing love from the most amazing woman. The only woman he could envisage having permanently in his life. The only woman with whom he wanted a future.

Zoey *was* his future.

Zoey decided there was no more painful thing than watching one of your best friends get married, knowing you would never experience the same exhilarating joy. It was a month since she'd left Finn in Monte Carlo and, apart from the odd email or text message regarding business issues, she had not seen him in person.

Zoey listened as Ivy and Louis exchanged vows under an archway festooned with white and soft pink roses. The love they felt for each other was written all over their glowing faces, both of their voices poignantly catching over the words, 'Till death do us part'. Zoey wasn't a habitual weeper but seeing such depth of emotion in the young couple made tears sting at the back of her eyes. She had so dearly hoped that one day she would stand exactly as Ivy was doing, exchanging vows with the man she loved with her whole heart. But instead, her heart was broken, shattered by the realisation Finn would never love her.

Zoey heard Millie begin to sniffle beside her, no

doubt eagerly awaiting her own wedding day the following month. But if there was anything positive to be had out of the pain of the last few weeks it was this—her father was in full-time residential rehab and his estranged wife Linda had been visiting him every day. It was wonderful to see her dad finally taking responsibility for his drinking and, while it would take a while for Zoey to feel close to him, she knew things were heading in the right direction.

Ivy and Louis's reception was a joyous affair and Zoey got swept up in the celebrations, determined not to allow her own misery to spoil her friends' special day.

'Time to throw the bridal bouquet!' the Master of Ceremonies announced. 'Single ladies, please gather in the centre of the room.'

Millie nudged Zoey. 'Go on. That means you.'

Zoey rolled her eyes. 'No way.'

Millie grabbed her by the arm and all but dragged her to where the other young women were eagerly assembled. 'Come on. Ivy wants you to be in the circle. And make sure you catch it.'

Why? There was only one man Zoey wanted to marry and he was the last man on earth who would ever ask her. But Millie had a particularly determined look in her eye, so Zoey stepped into the circle with a sigh of resignation. The band struck up a rousing melody to get everyone cheering and

Zoey had never felt more like a fish out of water. The other women were right into the spirit of the event, cheering and whooping and jumping up and down, arms in the air, hoping for Ivy's bouquet to come their way.

Zoey, on the other hand, was trying to hide behind a larger woman, hoping to avoid the floral missile. The drum roll sounded, the women in the centre of the room became almost hysterically excited and Zoey closed her eyes, figuring she wouldn't catch the bouquet if she couldn't see it. But then something soft and fragrant hit her in the face and she reflexively caught it in her hands. She stared at the bouquet she was holding while the crowd cheered and clapped around her.

But she had never felt so miserable in her life.

Zoey finally managed to escape all the noise and cheering by slipping out of the venue to the garden, where there was a summer house covered in a rambling pink clematis. She sat on the padded seat inside the summer house and looked at the bouquet still in her hands.

'I'm really glad you caught that,' Finn O'Connell said, stepping out of the shadows.

Zoey blinked as if she was seeing things. The way her heart was carrying on, he might as well have been a ghost. 'Finn? What are you doing here? I didn't know you were invited.'

'I gate-crashed,' he said with an inscrutable

smile. 'May I join you?' He indicated the bench seat she was sitting on.

Zoey shoved a little further along the seat, the bouquet still in her hands—or at least what was left of it. She had been shredding it without realising, the petals falling like confetti around her. Her pulse was thumping at the sight of him, her senses reeling at his closeness. 'Why are you here?' She gave him a sideways glance. 'It's not very polite to gate-crash someone's wedding. If it's a business matter, then surely it could have waited?'

He removed the now sad-looking bouquet from her hands and set it to one side. 'It is a business matter—our business.' His dark gaze held hers in a tender lock. 'Zoey, my darling, I have come to realise what a damn fool I've been. I've been fighting my feelings for you for months, even before we got involved. But I was too frightened to admit it even to myself, let alone to you.'

He took her hands in both of his. 'I love you madly, deeply, crazily. My life is empty without you. Just ask Tolstoy. He's witnessed every miserable minute of me moping about my house for the last month. Please forgive me for not telling you sooner. For not realising it sooner.'

Zoey swallowed, her heart beating so hard and fast, she felt light-headed. 'I can't believe I'm hearing this…' Her voice came out as a shocked whisper. Shocked but delighted.

He gave a self-deprecating smile. 'I can't believe I'm saying it. I never thought I would fall in love with anyone. I didn't think I had the ability to until I met you. But you are the most wonderful person and I can't imagine being without you. Please say you'll marry me.'

'You want to get married?' Zoey gasped.

Finn got off the bench and knelt down in front of her, holding her hands in his. His eyes looked suspiciously moist, and her heart swelled until she could barely take a breath. 'My darling Zoey, will you marry me and make me the happiest of men?'

She threw her arms around him with a happy sob. 'Oh, Finn, I will, I will, I will. I love you, love you, love you, love you.'

Finn rose from the floor of the summer house, bringing her to stand upright with him. His arms came round her, his expression as joyful as her own. 'I love you so much. I will never get tired of saying it. I want you to come back and work with me. I want your name as well as mine on the letterhead. We'll hyphenate them—Brackenfield-O'Connell Advertising. It's got quite a ring to it, hasn't it?'

'You mean you don't want me to change my name to yours after we get married?'

His arms tightened around her. 'I don't want to change anything about you, my darling girl.'

'Oh, Finn, I never thought I could be so happy,'

Zoey said, gazing up into his eyes. 'Being at Ivy and Louis's wedding has been like torture. Seeing them so happy made me realise how miserable I was without you. And when I accidentally caught the bouquet just then, I wanted to curl up and hide. Millie just about frogmarched me out there to join in. I thought it was a little mean of her at the time, because she knows how unhappy I've been.'

Finn's eyes began to twinkle. 'I heard she's a fabulous jewellery designer. Do you think she'll design our rings for us? She seems the most helpful and obliging sort of person.'

Zoey's eyes widened. 'Oh, my God, she knew you were going to propose! No wonder that bouquet came straight at me. She made sure it did. But she's normally hopeless at keeping a secret.'

He grinned. 'I might have mentioned to her I was dropping by to see you.' He brought his mouth down to hers in a lingering kiss. He finally lifted his mouth off hers to smile down at her. 'How soon can we get married? I don't want to wait for months on end.'

'Nor do I,' Zoey said. 'But I thought you never wanted to get married. And what about kids?'

'I never envisaged making a family with anyone before I met you,' he said. 'But the idea is increasingly appealing. I bet you'll be the most beautiful mother in the world.'

'And you the most amazing father,' Zoey said.

'Speaking of fathers…did you know my dad has been in rehab for the past month? He's doing really well so far.'

'I'm really glad for you and for him,' Finn said. 'And I've even thought of contacting my parents to ask them about their backgrounds. You got me thinking that there may be more to their behaviour than I thought.'

He brought her even closer, his gaze tender. 'You have taught me so much about love and caring about people. I found it near impossible to trim down the staff from Brackenfield in the takeover.'

Zoey hugged him again. 'I'm glad you found your heart. I knew it was there inside you somewhere.'

He tipped up her face to look deeply into her eyes. 'It was there waiting for you, my darling.'

* * * * *

Blown away by One Hot New York Night*?*
You're sure to be captivated by the
first and second instalments in
the Wanted: A Billionaire trilogy:

One Night on the Virgin's Terms
Breaking the Playboy's Rules

Why not also explore these other stories
by Melanie Milburne?

Billionaire's Wife on Paper
The Return of Her Billionaire Husband
His Innocent's Passionate Awakening

All available now!

COMING NEXT MONTH FROM

HARLEQUIN

PRESENTS

Available April 27, 2021

#3905 PREGNANT WITH HIS MAJESTY'S HEIR

by Annie West

One reckless night with an unforgettable stranger leaves Aurélie expecting! She's scandalized to discover her baby's father is new king Lucien! Now she must confess all to the reluctant royal and await His Majesty's reaction...

#3906 THE RING THE SPANIARD GAVE HER

by Lynne Graham

Accepting billionaire Ruy's convenient proposal rescues innocent Suzy from a disastrous marriage...and creates a major problem: their raging chemistry! He's all icy control to her impulsive emotion. Soon returning his temporary ring feels like the biggest challenge of all...

#3907 CINDERELLA'S NIGHT IN VENICE

Signed, Sealed...Seduced

by Clare Connelly

When Ares insists shy Bea accompany him to a gala, she wants to refuse. The gorgeous Greek is as arrogant as he is charming, yet she can't say no to her PR firm's biggest client...or to one magical night in Venice!

#3908 HER DEAL WITH THE GREEK DEVIL

Rich, Ruthless & Greek

by Caitlin Crews

Virgin Molly knows the danger of walking into a powerful man's den. Yet only an outrageous deal with Greek billionaire Constantine will save her beloved mother. He has always been sinfully seductive but, bound by their pact, Molly burns for him. And there's no going back...

HPCNMRA0421

#3909 THE FORBIDDEN INNOCENT'S BODYGUARD

Billion-Dollar Mediterranean Brides

by Michelle Smart

Elsa's always been off-limits to self-made billionaire Santi. Now as her temporary bodyguard he'll offer her every luxury and every protection. To offer any more would be the most dangerous—yet tempting—mistake!

#3910 HOW TO WIN THE WILD BILLIONAIRE

South Africa's Scandalous Billionaires

by Joss Wood

Bay needs the job of revamping Digby's luxurious Cape Town hotel to win custody of her orphaned niece. That means resisting their off-the-charts chemistry, which is made harder when Digby gives her control over if—and when—she'll give in to his oh-so-tempting advances...

#3911 STRANDED FOR ONE SCANDALOUS WEEK

Rebels, Brothers, Billionaires

by Natalie Anderson

When playboy Ash arrives at his New Zealand island mansion, he never expects to encounter innocent Merle and their red-hot attraction. He's back for one week to lay his past to rest. Might he find solace in Merle instead...?

#3912 PROMOTED TO THE ITALIAN'S FIANCÉE

Secrets of the Stowe Family

by Cathy Williams

Heartbroken Izzy flees to California to reconnect with her past and finds herself in a business standoff with devastatingly handsome tycoon Gabriel. He's ready to bargain—if she first becomes nanny to his daughter...then his fake fiancée?
